Doctor Nobody and
the Lower Animals

Doctor Nobody and the Lower Animals

Schuy R. Weishaar

ROUNDFIRE
BOOKS

Winchester, UK
Washington, USA

First published by Roundfire Books, 2020
Roundfire Books is an imprint of John Hunt Publishing Ltd., No. 3 East St., Alresford,
Hampshire SO24 9EE, UK
office@jhpbooks.com
www.johnhuntpublishing.com
www.roundfire-books.com

For distributor details and how to order please visit the 'Ordering' section on our website.

Text copyright: Schuy R. Weishaar 2019

ISBN: 978 1 78904 413 3
978 1 78904 414 0 (ebook)
Library of Congress Control Number: 2019941563

A CIP catalogue record for this book is available from the British Library.

Design: Stuart Davies

UK: Printed and bound by CPI Group (UK) Ltd, Croydon, CR0 4YY
US: Printed and bound by Thomson-Shore, 7300 West Joy Road, Dexter, MI 48130

We operate a distinctive and ethical publishing philosophy in
all areas of our business, from our global network of authors to
production and worldwide distribution.

Other books by Schuy R. Weishaar:
Dark of the Center Line (ISBN-13: 978-1785352690)
Masters of the Grotesque: The Cinema of Tim Burton, Terry Gilliam, the Coen Brothers, and David Lynch (ISBN-13: 978-0786471867)

for Connie and Ronald Weishaar
Sound thinking is to listen well...

Acknowledgements

The author would like to thank Mark Woods, Araz Khiziryan, and Erica Luckenbach for their comments on earlier drafts of this book, as well as Kyle Weishaar, who read and annotated draft after draft after draft.

Thanks also to the Roundfire team.

Fear brings about repentance, and through repentance comes revelation of hidden things.
—St. Isaac the Syrian

Lord Rama looked quizzically at Hanuman and said, "What are you, a man or a monkey?"
Hanuman, folding his paws and bowing reverently, said, "When I do not know who I am, I serve you. When I know who I am, I am you."

All your buried corpses now begin to speak.
—James Baldwin

Chapter 1

Zero is the mark of the Fool in the tarot, the wild card, but zero is not exactly nothing. It's a something standing-in for where nothing should be, a nothing-something, an eclipse, that can replicate itself with any other number, but which, at the same time, really brings nothing new to light, though the nothing that it brings is something.

Zero is a circumscription of the void.

Consider this: zero forms the foundation around which the other numbers are built, on both the left and right. Zero is the nothing haunting the rest, reminding that each could always, at any moment, become nothing. As far as you may get from zero, you never leave it behind. Zero is the beginning and zero is the end. This is why the perfect zero should be a perfect circle, though neither is possible. There is no beginning and no end. The Buddhist meditation recalls this: zero equals infinity.

And so the Fool. We are all born fools, and we die fools, knowing nothing. We build on the foundation of our foolishness, and this foolishness haunts us. In the tarot image marked "The Fool," the figure's gaze is fixed on the heavens, the full sun in the yellow sky behind him. Some have described him as sun-drunk, driven mad by divine revelation: the holy fool. They say he is powerless to stop the nipping of the wolf and dog, lost as he is in a reverie, about to wander off the precipice to his death. Soon, they say, he will be dashed against the rocks or drowned in the sea below.

But the fool's lesson goes deeper. The fool forgets himself, perhaps, but the forgotten self is the only self worth keeping in mind. He is nothing. He is unknowing. All wisdom in the world preaches the negation of self, that each individual must be stripped back to zero, that you must become a child again, must be reborn, must forget yourself and enter once more into foolishness in order to reach enlightenment. To become the fool is to forget what you have come to know: the fictions you have taken for truths, the fictions you forgot were fictions, the fictions that you call knowledge, the fiction, too, that you know as yourself. There is nothing more essential than forgetting, than becoming the fool.

This is your zero-point, your beginning and your end. And mine. This is the beginning of wonder, the wonder only discovered in silence. The knowing self is astonished by revelation, by illumination. This is anxiety. Astonishment is born of the sudden acknowledgement that you will disappear, that the void is waiting, that zero is just around the corner, that you and all you know will come to naught. This is Pascal on the mountainside. Astonishment is the response of your recognition that the void without merely mirrors the void within. Another name for this astonishment is horror.

This is why the fool is rejected and ridiculed, why he has no place to lay his head. The world has reasoned away his truth because it is frightening. The fool is the sign and harbinger of zero, of void, of silence, of the nothing that I am in the center of the something that you are. Nothing can happen. But the fool, in becoming nothing, learns wonder. He alone knows that what he knows is nothing. He sees its splendor, its possibility. It is his light that shines in the Hermit's lamp.

The Hermit knows the light, sees by it. But the fool embodies it, is it. He sees it vibrating, spinning through all of creation from that mountaintop. He sees the magic of the Holy Ghost in the illumined darkness. He is leading the wolf and dog. He is not drunk. He is not dreaming. He will not be dashed to pieces. He will not drown. The rocks leap up to meet his feet. He makes the waters calm. He is about to step off the cliff and walk on air...

Excerpt from an anonymous letter to Fr. Wilhelm "Will" Sorge, St. Francis Parish

Feast of Saint Thomas the Apostle, 1988

Chapter 2

Like a dog to its vomit. That's the way I returned to Illinois. Maybe that means it was folly. I guess time will tell. You never know what's in the cards. What I do know is that this place had put something in me that I needed to get out, and once I thought I had done so, I felt the lack, the emptiness of it, a gap, and somehow longed to put it back. I had seen a good part of the country, but the texture of this place was fitted to the texture of my mind. You would laugh at that if you knew this spot because it is as flat as a parking lot, and maybe that captures it, the texture I'm getting at. Something that's like a nothing. Something basic. Something obvious, on the face of it anyway. But, deep down, it's something as spiritual and mysterious as a holy mountain, too. Something as ancient and merciless and indifferent as the glaciers that leveled this land.

In my trade, when the fool returns to his folly, it's got little to do with religion. It's called recidivism. What I'm talking about is not so different from that. But that's not so mysterious: you return to what you know. "As the deer panteth for the water, so my soul longeth," you know? Maybe what is mysterious is the love that draws you. Whatever it is that makes you pant. The desire. Who knows? We're all born early, broken, incomplete, inchoate. Unfortunate animals. That's the human condition: we're never quite there. Being human is aspirational. Hilarious.

Love is what brought me back here. It's not what you're thinking. Probably just the reverse. I'm not going to spill it here. I'll just say this: love is powerful. It's Chernobyl powerful. The problem is it's as volatile as it is productive. It can drive a man for years, but once the conditions are agitated, and it's out of control, there is little else to be done than evacuate, build a fence, lower a dome, and keep out. Let time work on it until everyone's dead and God has filled it with wild nature, only ruins of that human failure poking out through the foliage. Only ghosts. Back when I was chief, I got a call to a hostage situation on the edge of town, out at Early McCurdy's place. That's what Mil had called it over dispatch anyway. A "hostage situation." The problem was simpler. The hostage and his captor were the same man. Early's kid, E.J., had locked himself in the bathroom with a pistol and called the station, talking about himself, but in the third person, hence the confusion.

The kid had always been screwy, and he'd crossed my path a few times for drunk and disorderlies, an assault here, vandalism there. He was rough. This time, though, he had reached the end of his rope. With help from something in a pill, a spoon, a needle, a pipe, or a powder, a kid finds the end of his rope like quicksilver around here. He'd made up his mind to kill himself. Maybe he was the first. I don't know.

I've worked in cities, and we had protocols for this sort of thing, but in a small town, where you've got too few to deal with it all, you just have to do the best you can. When Early's Ford stuttered into the yard, I'd been standing on a lawn chair with my head poked through the bathroom window trying to talk E.J.'s gun away for a quarter-hour without much hope. I had run out of arguments, and I've never been the sort of man who inspires people to see the bright side. Mil had called his dad at work and told him the business.

Early comes huffing across the grass like a wary rhino. He's got giraffe spots of black grease all over his red T-shirt, another one on his forehead, sweat hanging on the corners of the uneven handlebars of his mustache. I meet him at the door.

"Hop," he says, "don't you get in my way."

He puffs himself up the way a silverback does, thumping his beer keg chest, fizzing words at me.

I put my hands up. I was happy to see him. I let him pass. I figure if anybody can deal with a boy, it's his daddy. He flings the screen door open and charges in, cocked forward at the waist, head down, horn first. I go to the car, call Mil on the radio, taking my time, before I go back to the window. I heard it all happening. It doesn't take much imagination to see it.

Early grabs the kid by the hair, takes the gun, and fires it into the floor till it's just clicking. He's spewing curses. There are yells, cries, whimpers that accompany the soundtrack of combat. I'm thinking it's over.

Not so.

Early beats that boy every which way but straight, hooting and growling the whole time. Beats him till the screaming stops. I'm on the porch, thinking it's time to get involved before he kills that boy.

Too late.

By the time I get in there, E.J.'s head looks like some kind of potluck Jell-o dish. Early's knuckle bones are smiling out through his red, shredded skin. Looks like he's wearing butcher's boots. The boy he'd cradled when his momma died, taught to ride a bicycle, bailed out of jail for the same sorts of trouble Early himself had been in, is a dead pile in a pool of his own juices on the carpet. Early's still fuming explanations and warnings, not recognizing what he's done.

Love is a powerful thing. A dangerous thing. There's good and bad in everybody, maybe. But as soon as you lose sight of yourself, stop thinking for a split second, the one turns into the other. You might say, "Oh, come on now, Hop, that's just a vile man. An isolated incident."

Truth is, Early McCurdy was about as good as they come. He just loved that boy too much. But he loved him the wrong way round. He handled it like he would a hostage situation. Besides, haven't you ever seen some dumb brat wander into the street, only to have his daddy grab him back in a panic, and whip him right there on the curb, eyes flaring. Same damn thing. It may be that both are vile men, vile acts, but they're human, too. Too human. Or maybe just shy of it.

Somewhere, I read this little turn about rage: the root is poison, but the tip is honey. Is that not love in reverse? Maybe. But that doesn't mean it isn't still love. Love. Sick, human love.

Chapter 3

By the time Gordon Morris and his daughter moved back to town, I was a P.I. My primary client was the town itself. You might think that sounds like an odd arrangement. You'd be right. I served as chief of police for a while, but, as part of legal settlement with the town, and in order to avoid a conviction for sexual assault, I had to give up the badge. I kept the gun. The one I carried was my own.

Before I lose you, let me explain. First, it was "assault" according to a technical definition, but there was nothing sexual about it. In fact, the only kind of desire involved in the whole situation, while indeed animal, was intestinal. And it had to do with Mayor Rigby's boy, Kale.

As if Kale weren't a name stupid enough, yet fitting, for this moron, everybody called him Milky. God only knows why. What sort of man with a grain of dignity would answer when someone called, "Hey, Milky!" I just called him whatever vegetable came to mind when I saw him around the building. I called him dumbass, dipshit, you know, whatever the situation called for, but mostly I just landed on "the vegetable." He was an officer. He had about as much brains as a cannibal's turd. I could tell that from the first day. It takes either Christ's humility or the wits of a possum to write "unskilled worker" on a job application, and this man had none of the former.

Out here in the country, we didn't have police academies. It would help if you'd had some kind of experience in security or law enforcement, maybe time in the service, but what helped more than anything in those days was if your momma was the mayor. I put up with him, but I hated just about all there was to hate about him.

It was probably to the point where I hated certain things about him because they were about him. He rode a motorcycle. I hated motorcycles. He brought egg salad for lunch. I've not eaten an egg since. He came back from vacation with a mustache. I passed him in the doorway on my way to the barbers. I found myself watching him to discover new things to despise. He repulsed me. He was the sort of man who farts openly and then jokes about it, saying there must be a frog under his desk. It got to the point that I just had to ignore him. Like a cease and desist order to myself regarding the sheer fact of his existence.

* * *

I don't know how clinically accurate it is, but I'm told by people who know about this kind of thing (namely, my ex-wife, a psychologist at the college) that I have what I hesitate to call a condition, exactly. I suppose it's more of a peculiarity. They call it safe toilet syndrome. I call it rationality.

People are repulsive animals, and they're at their most repulsive and most bestial when they're in a bathroom. Just take a few minutes and observe any public toilet, and you'll see what I mean. God help you if you can stomach it all. The farting, spitting, pissing, nose-picking, wiping, jiggling, dripping, and that's not even to mention feces. Worse, still, is the exhibition, or lack thereof, of hygienic practices. It's more than a man can take, and, frankly, more than he should be asked to. The problem is, unless you're lucky or wealthy, you've got to be out in the world, which means you're bound to have to use a toilet that you've got little control over. But there's the thing: you do have just a little control. Especially if you're the chief.

It was May 31, 1986, a Saturday. I know the date because I heard it so many times in court proceedings (and because it was just shy of a week after that farcical exhibition, Hands Across America). When you're the police chief in a small town, you can't just call out of work over every little thing. I'd eaten something the previous night that, by sun up, had caused a storm, let's say.

On the morning of the thirty-first, I'd been on the toilet four times at home before arriving to the station at eight o'clock. My usual strategy, under ideal conditions, was to use the office toilets exclusively for the waterworks. Anything that required sitting and solid matter I saved for the house. Maybe I swung by at lunchtime or midafternoon. It wasn't a big deal.

On this particular day, however, these urges could not be suppressed for more than as long as it took to get from my desk to the bathroom with the cleaning supplies, spray the throne down with bleach, wipe it with a wadded glove of paper towels, wash my hands, and perch myself on the porcelain. This may seem to you overly fastidious, but, in my book, these are the actions of any sane human being. This is the control we have in a civilized society. Now, if you're in charge, you can also give orders that your men keep clear when they see you running. That's exactly what I did in the morning meeting.

Imagine my horror, my disbelief, my utter dismay, when, after high-tailing it to the bathroom, scrubbing the third stall (the one in the back, farthest from the door), while I was washing my hands, squeezing my buttocks together so hard my L5 popped, that damn vegetable walks past, whistling "Yankee Doodle Dandy," and into the third stall. He closes the door behind him, shucks his pants, and says, "It's sure a shame that I'm gonna hafta mess this up. It's like an operating theater in here."

I was speechless. I could feel the blood rise in my face like in those old cartoons.

He says, "Hey, Chief, why they call it an operating theater anyways?"

That's when I kick in the stall door, just in time to see the lanky freak wiping a booger on the wall by the toilet paper dispenser, the remnants of another sticking to his mustache, his eyes as big as cauliflower blossoms. I pull his shirt-tail over his head and drag him out, kick him in the ribs, and handcuff him to the water fountain pipes, out in the hall, his pants still around his ankles.

I charge back in there and have to hover over that bespattered seat as the storm has its way with me for the fifth time, while I hold the broken door shut. And a few minutes later, after I've recleaned everything, rewashed my hands, and given myself a chance to cool down, I come out the door and remember the handcuffed cucumber. And Mayor Rigby's there. Milky's lunch, in a brown paper bag, is just hitting the floor by her red pumps, the jingle bells on the door behind her still ringing her arrival, her eyes the image of her son's from just a few minutes before.

Anyhow, there was a case brought against me. The mayor threw a fit. (Adding the "sexual" to the assault charge was her idea.) There was a fair bit of snickering in the courtroom. (Officer Parsnip was not well liked around town.) It was covered in the local paper, where I was misquoted as saying, "Milky Rigby must possess the mythical Idiot Stone. He has the uncanny ability to turn everything around him to crap." It was close. I guess Tom Fulton at The Chronicler was sparing the public my more eloquent word choice. He did get the clincher right, though, about the kid being "a King Midas of morons."

It was a tempest in a tea pot, but, along with the old skeletons of "mental instability" they'd dug up on me from a while back, around the time of the divorce, it was enough to get me fired, of course. The kid stayed on the force for a while before, more or less, disappearing. His mom, who refused to let up, alienated her base with her lack of good humor and was defeated the following year by Wayne Burnham, a friend of mine from the old days and, as it happened, my lawyer. I went into business for myself with Hopkins Carver, Private Investigation. It was Burnham's idea. So were the municipal contracts. Between work for his law office and for the town P.D., I earned a decent enough living.

Chapter 4

All that was before everything started happening, before all the suicides, the girl, and the rest of it. Before we took notice anyway. The thing about law enforcement, investigative work, too, is that you're always behind. This is true in a practical sense, but it's also true in an almost existential way. The system knows this. That's why it has to gather evidence, make arguments, consider how much doubt is reasonable. All of these steps are proofs that it is lagging behind. That, in the scope of civil society, it is always losing. The best it can do is adjudicate and punish. That may be a poor picture of justice, but that's about the only picture there is. Only very rarely do we stop a crime in medias res, as it were. When we do, the term "hero" gets thrown around, but even that is a celebration of losing, of missing where someone went off the rails, saw some weakness to exploit. That's just the way it is.

Take my town. You could track a kid. You look at his family. You track his proclivities since birth, how his parents treated him, how his friendships shake out, and on and on. You can say with relative certainty, "This kid is going to break the law." Hell, I've done it. I've called lots of them, and they didn't disappoint. But if I had acted on it, then I would have been the criminal. Do you see? This is the paradox. Where does it start? Who knows? You only know when you begin to notice, and even that is a projection backwards, something you can only identify later. Like in those old noir films. You wonder why there's always a voiceover talking about the beginning from the perspective of the end? It's because you never know where the start is at the start. You only see it after it runs its course.

So, where do I start? I guess with the Morris girl. Burnham had me brought in. Must've been a couple of days after they'd found her. Burnham, technically, didn't have any real, day-to-day authority over the department, but the chief, a man named

Carter, deferred to him. They sent me long-view, investigative stuff, and they brought me in when they were in over their heads in something. Most of the force was locals who'd never been out of the area. Carter had been a cop in Champaign-Urbana for a stint, but that's only a slightly bigger pond, and he must not have been too big a fish there or else he probably wouldn't have ended up back here. Or maybe he just wanted a quieter life. Maybe he got in trouble. He was a good man as far as I knew him.

The short version is this: the girl was found dead in the basement of an abandoned house, one way out, a couple of miles from anybody else's.

* * *

I don't know how much difference it makes, but this was one of those old houses with a reputation. I'd been out there on a couple of occasions over the years. The first time was to investigate a huge skein of ducks that had died, apparently, almost all at once, in the front yard of the place.

An old lady got herself turned around somewhere, looking for a filling station to gas up at. She'd been on the interstate. Not a local. It was wintertime. I guess she was something of an amateur ornithologist or something. She sees all these ducks. (Seemed like a couple of hundred. I don't remember the final count.) She pulls over and gets out. She's standing there in the gravel on the shoulder with her binoculars. (Birdwatchers are their own breed with their own equipment.) She said it "took her aback," since the ducks, she said, should have migrated by then. And their "formation was off." (Her words. No idea.) Anyway, she's out there watching them, and the whole cloud of them veers off course and is heading right for her, like something out of Hitchcock. She starts off across the yard, which is frozen, of course, and the grass is dead, but high. She's going at full speed (which, as you might imagine, given her age, is probably not so fast), and she hits the deck. She says they swoop down, just over her. She looks back, thinking the whole thing's over, and sees them fly straight up. Next thing she knows, the whole lot of them are slamming into the ground all around her, some of them slamming into her. The last of them, she says, dive-bombs her backside, rolls off, shakes its little head around, takes off again, disappears into the sky, only to hit the hard ground right next to her head ninety seconds later. She watched the light go out of its eyes. She watched its neck swell up post-mortem.

There was the same sort of thing with a few dozen deer in the fall, except singles and doubles (that is, not all at once, like with the ducks). They seemed to wait for headlights out there, in front of the same damn house, and then charge at them from the yard: cars, trucks, whatever. There were even two little fawns that had it out with a man on a bicycle. I saw the bike. One hit the frame hard enough on the first try to daze himself before wobbling into the other lane, where he was hit by a grain-hauler and splattered all over the cyclist in the ditch. The other ended up strangling himself, ramming his head between the bike spokes and running away, dragging the bike into the trees. (That was a bad year for deer, but still.) It got to where no one drove that stretch of road for fear of running into psychotic, suicidal wildlife.

My role in these incidents was, more or less, to look around, bring out a veterinary research crew from the college in the next town over, and then assemble a few farmers with backhoes to help me bury the animals. I'm on a restricted diet, but people were even too afraid to eat the venison. Seemed like a waste. But what do you do?

I did a little research on the property. There was one article in The Chronicler, as far back as 1914, about a man, Vernon Hopper (everybody still called it "the Hopper house"), who farmed the place then. He had been killed in a barn there by an army of vermin—skunks, rats, coons—after he had sealed the escapes, blocked the doors, and made his last stand, armed with a pitchfork, two pistols, and bucket of pepper-juice. There were also rumors of aliens and hauntings and other such nonsense, from the forties through the sixties, which drew the weirdoes, then the hippies, and the teenaged Satanist-types for a time during the seventies. And the thrill-seekers among the young would dare each other to spend the night there. That sort of thing.

The point is the place had a history. So, while it was horrible and all, this event with the Morris girl didn't surprise folks much, especially with the spate of young people offing themselves, the way it would've otherwise, I mean. We don't get murders around here much (even McCurdy's case was pled down to manslaughter), and it wasn't clear that this was one either. It wasn't a "shock to the community," which was how they described it on the news in the cities. This was more of one of those "I knew it was just a matter of time" sort of stories. And people here being as they are, gossip floated around about the girl herself. She was a black kid. This is a white town. I mean that literally. Of everyone in the town, she was the only non-white resident. And people had ideas about that.

Inside, the place wasn't bad. It wasn't scary-looking. It had been remodeled in the early '80s. Nobody had lived there in a while. I got in touch with the owner in Wisconsin, a place called Cambria. She said she'd never seen the place. She had bought it for her son. He had worked on it, planned on living there. She said he had disappeared around Christmas the year before, out on a walk around Tarrant Lake, there, near her place in Cambria. Probably, he'd fallen through the ice or something. Never found his body though. She didn't know what to do with the house, but she was sorry about the girl.

The place seemed to have become a party house, and it looked like somebody had used one side of it for target-practice. There were beer bottles, cigarette butts, half-burned soda cans modified for smoking something, hundreds of little glass vials, bullet-holes and shell casings, and broken windows. Swastikas and whatnot spray-painted on the walls. They'd found her in the basement. It had been months since she'd first been reported missing, so she was pretty far gone when the kids found her. A couple of fifth-graders had gone exploring. (Like I said, this was that kind of place.) One of them bumped something when he was hiding in a kitchen cupboard, planning on scaring the other one. It released a drop-down door, like you'd see for an attic trap, except with a custom half-ladder, so it didn't have to fold; it just closed flush against the floor, between the joists. Looked like a bomb shelter type of thing, though Carter, the chief, said they were calling them "safe rooms" now (the paranoia sticks around; the nomenclature changes). The boys bolted when they spotted her.

Carter and company wrote it up. They concluded that the kid had probably been out there fooling around, too, that she'd hit the switch, had gone down to the safe room, and kicked the other one by accident in the dark, and couldn't find it later. Maybe she hadn't even realized that she was the one that closed the door. It was plausible. I tested it. It even looked like the safe room switch was built to be activated by foot, though it was hidden under the bottom of a metal-wire shelf. She had tried to escape. There were some fence-posts out in the floor and some indentations on the bottom of the door, where it looked like she'd tried to ram it. There was a window, made of that glass brick stuff. It was cracked, but that stuff is thick as hell. Carter said they'd just found her curled up on an old church pew, like she'd fallen asleep at a slumber party, playing with some tarot cards, the Hermit face up on the deck, the Fool still in her hand. The coroner said she'd probably just starved to death. Said he would've called her at sixty-five to seventy-five pounds when she'd died. She was five and a half feet tall. She turned seventeen years old while she was in the ether. Two things looked off, he said. One was some cuts around her mouth. (He found a tiny sliver of glass in one of them.) The other was that her wrists were broken.

Chapter 5

I'd heard about this through Burnham first, since Carter had asked him to break the news to the Morris kid's dad, Gordon, who I knew a little. The rest came later on, after I'd gotten more involved. Carter called somewhere around there, asking, would I talk to the priest, Father Will, down at St. Francis? Wasn't sure what it was about, but between this thing with the Morris girl and some trouble with a gaggle of redneck skinheads at the high school, they were backed up. I told him I would.

Father Will had been the priest since I moved here with my mom when I was a kid, and he seemed old then. St. Francis was my parish when I felt Catholic enough to go to mass, and we'd always got on real good. I asked him once if he really believed in transubstantiation, you know, that the bread and wine actually becomes the body and blood of Christ. He said it seemed more plausible than the Protestant idea that the congregation itself could be transformed into anything worthwhile. He was that kind of priest. He was waiting for me in the parking lot when I pulled in. Comes up to the window.

"Hopkins, I have some concerns," he says. "I've received a letter. Thought I'd call Carter. That it might be something."

I tell him okay. He hands me the letter. It's long, pages and pages of slanted print on unlined yellow paper. He lights up. I see his hand shaking when he drags on the cigarette. I'd received communion from those hands hundreds of times and never seen a quiver. I find my glasses and read the letter on the steering wheel.

* * *

Dear Father Will,
I am The Hermit. (Triple three is nine, the holiest number.) I

17

am a man, a man old enough to know some things, on a walk with my staff and light at night. It's summer, the solstice, perhaps, I don't know. There's a full moon. This coincidence happens maybe twice in a century. That's what they say anyway, the people who track the movements, the patterns, the ones who follow time. I keep my memories away, to keep the waters calm. You said that once, told me to keep the waters calm. Your very words.

It's a clear night. Two dogs stand by the water. A few smoky clouds wind around, black shadow-clouds; they glow low moonlight. It's late, but the moon is still low. It hangs like something artificial, something from a painting. But, since it's low, we see it through the heavier air, with its haze of invisible particles, so it's red, or amber, rather.

The man is limping. I am. I am limping. I am the man, remember, his voice anyway. Maybe more, though I can't say for sure. But I am at least a voice. It's not something you'd notice if you weren't really watching him, the limp, that is, but it's there. He's very thin, but he's sturdy-looking, not frail. I am, from far away, seeing from the outside, the way you do, the way you could if you wanted to. He's dressed in black jeans and a dark button-up shirt, long-sleeved, plaid. His hair is gray, curling above his collar. His beard is black with gray. With his hands in his pockets, he walks on, lowly whistling Bach; it's a cello suite, the first one, my favorite. After a while, this trails off, and then he is quiet as he continues toward the lake.

I can often be seen walking the lake. I'm not sure anyone takes notice. I would notice though, if I were on the outside, watching.

Imagine it: he makes his way, murmuring something to himself as his night-walk takes him down to the docks. It continues, only pausing briefly as he says hello to a man he passes on his way to the boat he is going to steal—the boat that I stole.

He boards it, starts the engine, and begins taxiing backwards, cutting the wheel to the left, pointing the nose toward the open water. I ease the boat forward and away from the docks. Someone is calling out to him, to me, to himself maybe, or for his own sake anyway. Now cursing. There's another voice. Do you hear it? The voice is lost in the wind-noise. A woman on the shore looks up as water trickles down from a dish in her hand. Why not? She's the image of The Star. Seventeen. Shall we pull back? So you can watch it from a middle distance?

The man on the boat is going so slowly across the water that the boat almost oozes forward. That's how it looks from the outside. The boat and its captain, its single passenger, move through the amber ribbon of light from the enormous pocked and pinking moon. Can you see him for an instant there before he passes? Light smears across his shoulders, his head. A smear of a man on a red horizon. His wide, black eyes blinking at his destination. Light on the water breaks in the boat's wake. The ripples spread shimmers outward from the center-point of the beam, a million fireflies loosening ranks, and just when it seems the light may be so agitated that it will dissipate altogether, the water calms, and the smooth ribbon returns, gentle flames playing, twinkling here and there, with subtle undulations of the water. He is a dark speck on a horizon where, now, the deepest blue meets black. And then it's like he was never there. Perhaps I never was. Perhaps I was only a dream, a nothing within you.

Father, now that the sun has set and the moon is out, I see myself in the evening light and recognize that I am alone. I have always been alone. You will remember this, should you try hard enough. Perhaps you've already discovered it. I'll leave that mystery to you. Anyway, that is not why I am writing. I am writing to you, Father, because, as I said, I am alone.

I know what kind of priest you are, and more, what kind of man you are. If you are reading this, then I am dead. Or I have given it on a whim, or there has been some mistake or change in my plans. Anything is possible. Maybe I'm just gone. Somewhere. I am not sure what I will do from one day to the next or where the world will carry me. You may absolve me in absentia; you may call down God's wrath upon me; you may pass this document on to the authorities. Whatever you wish. I tend to think you will bless me and pray for me, but the choice is yours.

We are alone, Father, you and I. In different ways and to varying degrees, of course, but we have this in common. That we live in a sacralized cosmos superimposed on a secular age, a desacralized age. This makes us alone. I know you believe that each time you say mass, the body and blood are real. I could see it in your eyes when the bell was rung. And this in an age when even bishops assume it's only ritual. But they believe in the abstractions of mathematicians, in the parallel universes of quantum physicists. Perhaps they are better Platonists than Catholics. It would terrify them to think they had really touched the divine. Or worse, that they had been experiencing it for years without realizing it, without sensing that it was real. They would be as worried that it would give them cancer as that it might make them holy. It is, though, a terrifying realization.

Imagine it with me, Father. Above the lake, the moon, almost imperceptibly, ascends and shrinks at once, lightening with every inch, as it slowly swings away from the earth, as the order of things keeps its time. And somewhere between pale pink and muddy yellow, I will wake up and remember nothing. Remember that I am nothing.

And in this instant you will too. You will wake to nothing.

Nothing sacred. You will put this paper down and be left in the emptiness.

Only an image will remain, two images, rather, conjoined as one. But we will only remember the one: an eclipse, a radiant, cosmic zero, the nothing that I am at the center of the something that you are. But, as Rilke says,

Nothing can happen. All things come and circle
constantly round the Holy Ghost,
round the certain spirit...

* * *

This first letter seemed like a lot of crazy talk to me, and I wasn't sure what Father Will wanted me, or Carter, or anybody else to do about it. I asked the usual questions: How'd you get it? Who'd it come from? And so on. He had no idea. It had just shown up in the box at the church. But it bothered him. "Concerned him, deeply," was the way he kept saying it.

"For now," I said, "just put it somewhere safe. Hold on to it. Think on it, and if you remember anything, or if you can decode any of this nonsense, then you know how to get ahold of me."

He agreed, nodding, rubbing the bridge of his nose between his finger and thumb.

"Let's not bother Carter with it for now," I said, "since, apparently he's neck-deep in Nazis."

"Oh dear," he said.

He was deeply concerned.

Chapter 6

This is a small town. And, to look at, at first anyway, The Society was not a scary crew. They looked like the rest of the kids around here: like farm boys, like kids you'd see at the high school football games, in the stands or on the field, like kids whose pictures you'd see in the local paper for something good. Most of them were young, teens and twenties, maybe a few older than that. Some had put in time in colleges. The point is they didn't put fear in people the way the others, the ARAFO, did. The Society were mostly locals. I knew a lot of them individually, knew their families, but the group was new, even if the ideology and haircut weren't so novel.

This is the Land of Lincoln. You see that all over the place. People think of the South when they think of the Klan, maybe of the East Coast when they think of skinheads. I don't know. Here's the thing though. When you drive out of a city, like Chicago, say, and into the rest of the state, the little towns you've never heard of, like this one, you go back in time. That has its sentimental appeal for some, but go and drive through those small towns, eat in the diners, gas up at the filling stations, and it's like Mayberry. The locals will wave. Your waitress will smile. The children will laugh. The cop will stop and help you change a flat. You'll see the mayor weeding the flowerbed at the courthouse. But just like Mayberry, they're all white people, white people who have never said more than two words to man, woman, or child who isn't.

That sort of thing comes from somewhere.

* * *

I was born in Chicago. The only daddy I ever knew was a black man, Hopkins Carver, the first. I don't know the white man who raped my mom on her way home from class at the University of Chicago, causing me to be born nine months later. (Mom's family was Catholic, so certain options were off the table.) But the man I called dad gave me his name as my own, loved me, fed me, taught me, and in a lot of ways made me who I am. I was seventeen when he was shot four times, twice in a leg, twice in the back, by a white cop in '68, during the riots.

Mayor Daley had given the order to "shoot to maim or cripple anyone looting any stores in our city." And this officer saw a black man with a leather briefcase and a London Fog trench coat, a black man with a nice coat, an expensive bag, carrying a box, and thought the worst. He'd never seen a black lawyer, I guess. Shot him in the leg from behind. My father fell on the sidewalk, books tumbling from the box in his arms. The cop put two more in him when he was down, afraid he was reaching for a gun. He died in the hospital from an infection. I think the government count of casualties during the riots was twelve or fifteen, which is pretty good, considering. But my father was not included in that reckoning. And how many others?

My mom fell apart, and we ended up back here, where she'd grown up, living with her grandmother (her parents had died in a car crash a few years before). No one knew, no one asked, she couldn't talk about it, and I was too angry to. They took us in, the town, I mean. They were good to us. I wonder, though, if they had known, if things would've been the same.

* * *

What people here know of black people, "the blacks," as they call them, comes mostly through the television. Some, who have jobs in bigger towns nearby, have polite interactions at work, and whatnot, but, to them, these are the exceptions. On the news, after Malcolm X, after Martin Luther King, black people were The Panthers.

J. Edgar Hoover told them, the Black Panthers were the greatest internal threat to the nation. Think about that. That's the FBI director, during the Cold War with the Soviets, during the hot one in Vietnam. The sad part is people here believed it. He was saying what they were already translating out of the static in their heads. When they heard Fred Hampton was machine gunned to death, they were relieved. It didn't matter that he was in bed asleep when it happened.

Guns around here were like instruments in the marching band. People walked around with them, had them displayed in their trucks in parking lots. They were a rite of passage for boys. Hell, most girls could shoot. It wasn't The Panthers' guns that scared people, not the people here anyway.

I think it was the confidence. Think about it. If you'd have asked them, people would say it was the aggressiveness, the anger, the sense of being owed something better than they'd worked for. But that's all code that they never took the time to decipher from their own emotional stenography.

I think it bothered them to see confidence dripping off of a people they didn't think were entitled to it. A people who used their black guns to police *their* (white) cops, a people who used their black voice to protest *their* (white) politics, a people who used their black logic to win over *their* (white) young to their causes. A people who thought they deserved the (white) freedom *they* had. A people who, by their very existence, threatened the (white) America *they* had enjoyed, the America that favored *them*. This was a people who wanted in on America, and they wouldn't even apologize for being black.

Then, when the tube had finished with The Panthers, when they weren't a threat anymore, it was Affirmative Action for blacks, black Farrakhan, a black mayor in Chicago, black gangs in big cities, black music, black drugs, the black church. But for people here, none of this could weave into a progressing narrative towards a future, a change. This is Mayberry, remember? And

Mayberry is a (white) fantasy of the past.

They believed Nixon, too, when he said Dr. Leary was the most dangerous man in America, just like they believed Hoover. Time stands still. The world comes in through the pictures moving on the glass, through the radio talking into your head in your car or your kitchen. This is the forties, the fifties maybe, and the onslaught of time outside, with its sixties and seventies (Ain't them hippies the same kids that rallied for Huey P. Newton? And against our boys in 'Nam?), pumps dread into people's minds like a drunken clown blowing fetid breath into a balloon at the state fair, like a tea kettle that can't whistle out the steam.

There is no "history in the making" here. It's only entropy. It's a poisoning, an infestation. Keep the world away. Time doesn't move inside the small town. But the pressure is always building, without a future to let it out. The world races around on the interstate, miles outside of town, on the news even farther, on the radio from somewhere. Everything is far away. The TV shows the world is going to hell, and we can't even see it, but, by God, not here. We think for ourselves. We know who's to blame. *They* are.

And "they" is anyone but "us."

* * *

Since 1908, the town hadn't had any but white residents, not until the Morris girl anyway. It's not something people talk about anymore. These days, of course, no one's alive from that time, but there was back in the '80s, when this all hit the fan. But even then, if you'd have asked people, they'd give you a frown, they'd look off somewhere far, they'd swing their heads, and say they didn't remember. You go to the library here, and they've got Chroniclers that go way back, but there are a few days in August of 1908 that you just can't find. You dig around enough, though, you can find just about anything.

It's an old story, a love story. A black man gets caught with a white woman, and the details are sketchy, so sketchy in this case that neither has a name, that the story breaks in whispers, in rumors, and grows in people's heads. You see? Always behind. How do you get out in front of something with a genesis that murky?

It grows and grows.

And then explodes.

You can still go and see the black neighborhood. The town is smaller now, and there's a field that separates it from where the town sits today. There are the footings where a bridge used to be, over the creek. There are broken brick-made chimneys. There's still a post for a street sign or for a horse maybe. Even a couple of basements. The rest was burned down. It's returned to the wild, grown over with a hundred years of trees, joined back to the woods that leads down to the flood plain where the river runs up. Not even a ghost town. Those that weren't hanged, beaten, shot, or burned to death never came back. There were no arrests. The whole debacle was committed by a mob of "persons unknown."

That kind of subterranean paranoiac hatred doesn't evaporate. It's not a mutation that disappears in the following generation. Maybe it's more like magma. It's always down there, under the surface, the pressure always changing. For a time, it's invisible. One day it comes boiling out, sets fire to everything in its path. But it also burns itself out, destroys itself, in the process. The return of the repressed.

A murder is just a misdirected suicide.

Chapter 7

I'm a reader. Never took myself to be too good to learn something. I've even taken some classes at the college. That's where I first met Dr. Morris, Gordon, the girl's daddy. Anyway, I read this book once by Sherwood Anderson, called *Winesburg, Ohio*, about a little town full of freaks, each with his own private desperation, hidden under the daytime smile, the squeeze of the hand, the cordial well-wishing. I think he just about nailed it down. People are here for two reasons. They're afraid of the world, so they never leave, or they've run here away from something, come here to lick their wounds. They're afraid the world's going to eat them up, or it already has.

What I'm getting at is the suicides. It took time to recognize them for what they were because it's not all that uncommon for a man to blow his brains out around here. I'd like to think that, were I still on the P.D. instead of hired help, I'd have noticed something, but I don't know that I would've. And from the outside, I'd read the obituaries like everyone else. Families don't exactly advertise that their loved ones shot, poisoned, electrocuted, or burned themselves to death out of despair, shame, loneliness, or what have you. They're "accidental deaths," and in farm country, where people do their own electrical work, where they hunt and play with guns, where most people don't pry (even if they may gossip), they're plausible. But only up to a point.

The one that got me thinking was the kid who died trying to climb a rope tied to the guardrail on the bridge over the interstate. Carter had called me in; they were working two others killed in gun-cleaning accidents the same week.

"Carter," I said, "We can't call this an accident. He stapled a note to his shirt. He built a perfect hangman's noose at the end of the rope, stuck his head in it, and jumped. Gravity was on his side. He wasn't fighting it. He wasn't climbing. His hands are soft as butter. It's plain as daylight. Suicide."

"Hop, just write it up. He might've meant the loop as a foothold and got tangled up."

I stared at him.

"That's not what the note says," I said finally.

"Are *you* gonna tell his parents?" his eyes flaring. "Write it up."

I did as I was told, but it bothered me. I spoke to Burnham. He asked me to poke around a bit, quietly. Told Carter to let me see files, pictures, and so on.

Of the thirty-two "accidental deaths" in the year or so prior, thirty looked to me like obvious suicides. I mean gun-in-the-mouth, head-in-the-oven, clothes-soaked-in-gasoline suicides. No question. Some left notes, some didn't. I talked to families, and most of them knew already, of course, and knew I wasn't one to gab, so they talked. They were worried, too. They suspected something. They just didn't know what. Stranger was the fact that all their stories were the same. As you might think, these kids, most under twenty-five, were depressed. They'd pulled away, sat in the dark, alone, hours on end. They'd disappear for a while. Then they turned angry, short, some violent. They bawled or growled. And when they did talk, they all seemed to say the same thing. That they needed somebody.

Now, this is delicate work, so I wasn't pushing to look around houses or in these kids' rooms. It was quiet, tender work. But three of the parents a little further on in their grief volunteered it. It's strange, but none of them had changed a thing, almost like, if they just closed the door on the room where their dead child had lived, somehow that kid wasn't all dead. Not quite. There was some husk of him there, hanging in the air, and it was better not to chase it out, even if the only thing left was a cloud of silent despair. Better than nothing.

After I found the vials in two of the rooms, I knew the third kid had to have them somewhere. It was a basement apartment. I had all but torn it apart while his mother watched.

"He had a car," the mother said. "The Chevette out there. Whatever you're looking for. It could be in there."

Glovebox. Might as well have been in plain sight. A box of Winstons, four vials packed in between the smokes. Two were empty, but, in the other two, maybe a teaspoon's worth of clear liquid in each. The mother watched, pulled her cardigan in across her chest, crossed her arms, like she had caught a chill.

"What is that?" she asked.

"Don't know. Can I take it with me?"

She nodded.

Chapter 8

"Do you understand that this is your prison?"

The smear of a man stood in front of me. Nothing was clear. Where the mouth would be moved when he spoke. He was mostly voice, deep, full of static. Everything was a cloudy red heat, except for the man, but he seemed made out of smoke or soot, pieces of him fogging off, floating away, winding back into him, reigniting, like embers spinning in the wind and burning again. A stick-man that couldn't hold himself together. I couldn't feel myself at all. I could only hear.

It's hard to explain, but I could see him in front of me, high up, like I was looking from the ground, and at the same time I could see from above, down there in the red haze, the smear of the stick-man, moving back and forth across the red ground in front of what looked like a felled buck, giant, on its side, a rack of antlers holding its head up.

"No?" He waited. "I did not think so. I do not expect you to respond. Not with any sense anyway. That is why you are here. Do you understand that? You can continue playing your games, but they will not help you. Only I can help you. Do you understand that?"

The shape paced back and forth. A spray of embers curled off his head, spun, spread, and settled back into his leg.

"Let me instruct you on the philosophy of the hunt. You are in the woods, you, the hunter. You have your rifle, and you consider: well, it is easy; I spot the deer, take aim, and kill."

A pause.

"It is not that easy. Do you know why? It is because you are not an animal. Because you have a rifle. It is because you belong to a civilization that has learned well, has learned efficiently, how to kill, that you have forgotten how to kill, how to hunt to kill. Anyone can kill, but to hunt requires a different set of skills.

It requires a shift in your paradigm of thought, of where you fit. You probably think man is at the top of the chain. You probably think you can hunt and kill what you please, and you are right. Man *does* belong to a civilization, and that civilization is bred to kill. And with your peers, with your equals, that is how it is done. You can walk up to a man in broad daylight, and you can kill him. You will not even have to chase him. You will not even have to *hunt* him. Do you see? Do you know why?"

Another pause. In the quiet, I heard an animal noise, like a distressed sheep. From above I watched the buck shift its head, antlers scraping the hot red earth.

"Because he is just like you. He is conditioned to believe that he, too, is at the top of the chain. The law keeps him safe. It is written into his consciousness. He is beyond the hunt. He trusts that. But to learn to hunt is to learn to see yourself objectively. Yes, you are at the top of the chain. Yes, you are an efficient killer. But when you walk into the forest, you are walking into a world of lesser creatures, of lesser minds, without civilization, all of them hunted, all of them prey, all of them alert to the minutest indication of threat, to the very scent of it. You, the predator, have to learn to see yourself as the predator, you see, but from the world of the prey. I do not care what part of the forest you are in, there is prey to be had. You just cannot see it. You cannot see it until it breaks the law of the hunted, when its fear dissolves and it peeks out from its hiding place, when its fear is insufficient, and its guard is down as it feeds: when it forgets its place under the order of things, under the law of the hunted. Do you understand?"

The smear descended. Another spray blew off its shoulder.

"You have forgotten your place under the order of things. If you could see it rightly, you would know with certainty that we are all still under the law of the hunted. Can you not see that? It is only that the terms of the game have changed. And it is a game. It is a deadly serious one, but it is a game, as it has always been. The law does not care about you, the order of things does not care about you, none of this would have cared about you."

Its arms seemed to wave around, demonstrating the all that did not care.

"It does not care about you because it does not even know you are there. But it is waiting. It is waiting just like the hunter. It is waiting and watching for one whose fear has dissolved, one who has forgotten his place. Do you know what that one is called?"

Again, a pause. I couldn't answer, and, as it turns out, I didn't know the answer anyway. The animal said nothing.

"That one is called *meat*. And meat is always alone in the world. The law waits for it like the hunter waits, both of them already savoring their prey because without it neither would exist. Not even me. But I am not alone. I am the hunter. I have you. But you do not have me because, to me, you are nothing. Until you move. Only I can help you because, in helping you, I ensure my own survival. But in order for me to help you, you must see reality. You must regain your fear. I can help you, but I can only help you if you learn to fear. You must learn to fear the order of things. And you must come to know that, insofar as you are concerned, I set the order of things because I am the order itself. For you, I am the law. There is no other. And until you come to fear me, I will not be able to help you. And when you have regained your fear, the hunt is on. That is the help I offer. The hunt. The Law. Meaning. In a word, Love."

The figure smeared, sprayed, and dissolved into the hot fog as the voice faded. The buck, the red ground, the fire cloud contracted in three jerking twists. And I know it makes zero sense, but the only way I can describe what happened next is that everything became math, and I moved into some invisible point in the distance, only to have it contain another universe of math patterned the same way. Over and over. I was alone. I was nauseous, and I couldn't stop. I thought I was being pulled apart.

* * *

I came to a few towns away, out in the country. My face was wet with tears and sweat and snot. I had vomited down my shirt. The front of the car was crumpled against a couple of trees, a deer pinned there too between the bumper and the tree trunk. It was the outside of some woods that edged a dirt road. It was on fire, all of it, the trees, the car, the grass, the animal. The deer was bellowing, only its head and antlers sweeping around as it burned, the rest of it already dead. I unbuckled the seatbelt and stumbled away. I thought about shooting the deer. But just as that hit me, I guess the fire got to the gas tank, and it exploded. It wasn't quite like in the movies, but my car was done for. And the animal wasn't moaning after that.

I didn't know where I was right away. I sat out there on a log, watching my car burn. This was back when only fat cats had cell phones and they were the size of car batteries. All at once, I realized that it was night. Someone had to have heard the car blow up or seen the flames and probably called it in. I tried to put myself back together for when whoever was coming got there.

I didn't know how much time I'd lost or what the hell had happened to me until I remembered the vials. One had broken, maybe when I got in the car, or hit the brakes too hard. I found the pieces when I reached into my pants pocket. The other vial was still intact. My hand came out bloody. I loosened my belt and reached down my pants to check the punctures on the top of my thigh. I was trying to tweeze a shard of glass out of the skin near my groin. Of course, that's when the buggy with the Amish showed up. I looked over my shoulder and saw their beards swiveling back and forth between them in the fire light. Generally, the Amish only speak when they have something to say, and that night they didn't say much. I crawled up onto the bench between them. Never before had I felt so much from the impersonal, almost anonymous contact of my shoulders with theirs. I felt like it was the only thing keeping me alive.

* * *

It took me almost a week to right myself after whatever that stuff did to me. The biggest hurdle, odd as it may sound, was not to drink the other ones, if that was even how it worked. The impact of just the tiny taste of experience I'd had was ridiculous. Searing but, in another way, numbing. Like nothing mattered because everything weighed me down with such raw hurt. A paradox, I know.

There's a line in Isaiah: "I am forgotten like the unremembered dead. I am like a dish that is broken." That's what it felt like: completely alone, alienated from everything and everyone. Whether I was or wasn't dead for a time, I don't know, but hearing that voice, that's what I wanted to be: dead, wiped away. I wanted to be breathing my last. I wanted it to put out the fire of that voice and the movement that came after.

They're not really comparable, but the only thing that comes close is the stupor that took me over when my wife told me she'd been sleeping with another man. You can get addicted to that feeling. The floor has given way, and you're falling down, and down, swinging to kill at anything that gets between you and the bottom. Maybe because the pain so obviously means so much. You get addicted to the falling, to the violence of lashing out. It becomes a big zero, and you're spiraling down inside it, down into nothing, and it's the only thing that means anything. As bad as it hurts, you fear the time when the pain will stop. You'd kill yourself to stop feeling it, and you'd kill yourself if you did. You're stuck in that freefall.

Chapter 9

When I got back, I had a sit-down at Bernice's with Burnham and Carter. They ordered breakfast. I drank coffee. (I still wasn't able to eat more than a few saltines.) The town seemed to be going to hell.

"Nazis? I saw the rally, but I didn't know they were Nazis. Just, you know, skinheads," Burnham said.

"Is there a difference?" I asked. "Maybe just the haircut."

Carter had been filling him in on The Society. They'd been trying to recruit kids at the high school, passing out fliers about plans for their master race. They'd also been harassing the Amish, out in the country. They'd run them off the road, burned a barn, crucified a German shepherd for some reason, whipped the heads off of some chickens with a belt or a bullwhip or something. There'd also been some scuffles with a gang of punker-types, skater kids, right on the square, who showed up in front of the courthouse in masks to protest the "Rally for Brotherhood" that had happened while I was out. The Society had taken to burning crosses (I don't know what it is with these types and crosses), one at the Mason Lodge, and another at St. Francis.

"They're not Nazis, exactly," Carter said. "Milky Rigby's mixed up with them somehow. He says they're not Nazis. He said a shaved head is just cleaner, but I don't know what that's supposed to mean."

"Can you trust a kumquat's opinion of the dirt?" I asked.

They just looked at me.

"What is it then, something like the Klan?"

"Something like that," Carter answered Burnham. "Definitely a racial angle to it."

"Then why are they picking on the Amish? They're the most true-blooded Germans I can think of."

This was all news to me. I sipped my coffee.

"Maybe it's a mistake to expect it to make sense, Wayne," I said.

"There are no black people here," Burnham said. His hands in that universal gesture of confusion. "Not unless you count the Morris girl, and not even her now for a while."

"Wait," I said, "Dr. Morris' daughter was black?"

"You never seen her?" Carter asked.

"No, I just knew him from class."

It hit me who the Morris at the Hopper house was.

"You take classes?" Carter again, looking from me to Burnham. "Ain't Morris a philosophy teacher? Hop, you take philosophy classes?"

Burnham laughed.

"Yeah." Then to Burnham. "If that's all true, I'd say it's mighty suspicious, wouldn't you? That the one black resident of this town ends up dead in the basement of a vacant house with swastikas spray-painted on the walls and drug litter all over it? And just as this group of yahoos goes public?"

"I'm just learning we've got a Nazi problem. I didn't see the connection. I've been preoccupied with visiting the families whose kids fell victim to accidents," Burnham said. He used his fingers to make quotation marks around the last word.

"Well, those seem to be on hiatus. It's been a full two weeks since Randall, the one that hung himself at the bridge," Carter said.

"Hanged," I said.

"What'd I say?"

"Hung."

"What's wrong with that?"

"Hang, as in by the neck until dead, is a regular verb."

"What's hung for then?"

"Bulls' balls and framed photographs."

Burnham laughed again.

"Alright, what's this about drugs?" Burnham said. "If we've

got these, these Nazis, and we can pin them on drugs, we can get rid of them, right?"

He looked at Carter.

"Yeah, but we've gotta have a sure connection. A few smoking cans ain't gonna do it."

"What about this?" I held up a vial. "There're hundreds of these things out at that house. I got two from one of our suicides."

"What the hell is that?" Burnham said.

"I don't know, but it's real bad."

Burnham understood. "That's what happened to you?"

I nodded. "I don't even know how. Broke in my pocket. I woke up and the world was on fire."

We got up. Headed outside.

"Hop, why don't you poke around, find out what's what with that shit in the vial," Burnham said. "Use the old cruiser. It doesn't have a rig, but it still goes. Then look into the Nazis, or whatever the hell they are, and find out what you can. And stop by Saint Francis. Check on Will. Mildred says he's been calling the station. You know how he is. Gets wound up about things. That cross set afire there couldn't't've been good for his blood pressure."

Carter said he'd go back out to the Hopper house and take another look and otherwise try to keep the town from splitting open at the seams.

Carter handed me a set of keys from the million on his belt.

"Do they call themselves Nazis, this day and age?" Burnham squinted.

I was thinking the same thing. We looked at Carter.

"The Society is what I keep hearing. I know they're linked up somehow with Reverend Hinckley."

"Oh God. Hinckley?" I said. "Well, I guess that tells me where to start."

* * *

I stopped on my way out of town to see Father Will, before going to visit a professor I knew at the college, somebody who maybe could tell me what was in the vials. I let myself in the church. He was sitting at his desk. His face was grim and gray, his glasses suspended on his forehead. He was rubbing his eyes with the heels of his hands, cigarette pinched between his fingers, when I knocked on the open door.

"I'm glad you came by, Hopkins. You heard about the cross-burning?"

"I did. Carter seems to think that Hinckley's wrapped up in this somehow."

"That wouldn't surprise me. He has always tended in that direction. But this sort of thing seems rather extreme, even for him."

"You alright, Will?"

"I've been a priest for a long time. I've seen this sort of thing before. There is nothing new under the sun."

"Seems like this sort of thing crawled out from under a rock."

"Yes. Well."

He looked at me for a minute.

"Hopkins, I've got something, another letter."

"Yeah?"

I guess he read the counterfeited interest on my face. He's a priest. That's part of the job.

"Hopkins, this one is bad. Just awful. Again, it just showed up. I don't know what to think. I just don't know."

His eyes got glassy. I thought he might cry. He put a closed fist to his mouth, stifling a sob. I didn't know what to make of that.

"That poor child," he said after a moment.

"Which one? What child?"

"The girl, Gordon's girl."

He handed me the new letter, another bunch of yellow pages rubber-banded to a manila envelope with the other one inside.

"Take them both. You'll want to keep them. Thank you for coming by, Hopkins."

"Of course, Will. I'll be in touch."

I turned to go. He walked me out. I got to the car, opened the door, tossed the letters on the passenger seat.

"Hopkins?" he said.

I looked back.

"Hopkins, you don't look well."

I nodded and waved.

"Yup," I said. "That is probably true. Guess I'm an open book to you, huh?"

Chapter 10

Dear Father Will,

A young man once sat on his porch and told this story, a daydream, a vision, to a woman.

Imagine a girl as she wakes. It's morning. Motes of dust shimmer in the blue glow from the window. She sits up on the wooden bench she's been sleeping on in a basement under a house which isn't the house she lives in. She's alone. She's hungry. She's been crying in her sleep. She reaches for the cards she found in a box down there the day before or the day before that, she can't remember which anymore. She closes her eyes, her legs crisscrossed, and she breathes in deeply as she shuffles the cards. There are twenty-two. Almost unconsciously, she draws the one from the top and sets it face up on the table beside her without looking at it. She lies back down on her side, almost asleep again, whispering "the fool" into the quiet, before her breathing becomes deeper, the breaths longer. She is out again.

She is right about the card.

Time goes by. She never did find anything to eat. And no one came to her rescue.

With her body were two documents, written in different hands, that melted away, dissolved into the air. The first was a narrative, probably the girl's own, about herself, but, as it were, from the outside. The man quoted it to the woman. He had been unable to forget it. He knew it word for word.

"Colette woke up and still nothing had happened. Nothing had changed. No one had found her. The window was darker. That was all. It wasn't a window exactly. Things would have been much easier if it had been. It was a gap in the stone foundation of the house where a proper window might have gone, but instead thick blue-tinted glass blocks had been cemented in. While they seemed unbreakable, they let the light in, but that was all. This window didn't open, and she couldn't see much out of it. The view was not so different from what the world looked like through a glass of water. She could make out night and day and the blued green of the cornfield and the color of the sky, but she only knew the green was corn and the blue, pink, bright, or black was sky by inference, because she knew how colors interacted and because she knew the world was there already. The window only gave glimmers. It made her think of her dad."

"Colette's dad was a philosopher, though not long after moving here, she had learned to say that he was a teacher. Other kids' dads were farmers or mechanics; they were bankers or they sold insurance or tractors or something. There weren't any other dads who were philosophers, and even her teachers couldn't seem to square the word 'philosopher' with the words 'job' or 'work' or 'occupation.' So she just said 'teacher.' It was simpler. It didn't require a whole conversation."

"In a similar way, she had learned to say that she was 'black,' rather than get into the details of why her skin was brown, why her dad's was white, and on and on. In a town so small in the middle of Illinois, where she was the only kid who was brown, she was 'black' anyway, she knew that. She could see it in her neighbors' faces and in the looks from the other kids at the school she went to in the next town over. 'Where's your mom?' 'Is she dead?' 'Your parents split up?' The questions kept coming, and Colette kept manufacturing economical half-truths to protect herself, to conceal, to elide, to simplify, simplify, simplify: truths designed to lie. Probably not what Thoreau had in mind."

"Her dad had always made philosophy seem so natural. He used to tell her that it was just thinking things through. He had told her about the Allegory of the Cave as a bedtime story when she was small. He'd made shadow puppets on the wall with his hands. It was like a fairy tale. She used to beg for that story. Now she would give just about anything to get out of it. But here she was, trapped, though not chained, thankfully, wondering about the reality of murky images on the wall. Yes, she took them to be glimmers, shadows in a way, of the world outside, a world she'd never really doubted the reality of, but this, too, was real. She was cut off from everything she'd become accustomed to, even the simple things: that the sky was there, that the earth was real, that what she saw or touched or smelled or tasted were things that would go on without her. And here she was: Colette in Plato's cave, not having tasted anything in days; Colette's existential nausea; Colette's *Notes from Underground*; Colette in Meursault's prison cell, rebuilding the world from memory; and, if this persisted, the Death of Colette Ilyich."

Maybe here the girl sputtered some combination of a laugh and a sob, and it bounced around the hard little room. She put down the pencil.

By the look of the window, it would be dark before long. She wiped her nose on her sleeve. She rubbed her palms into her eyes and took a few deep breaths. She sat up and laced her fingers across her lap and lightly closed her eyes again, a tear curling around her nose. *Don't lose it.* She calmed herself with a few more breaths. She thought out the room again, her eyes still closed. She thought it through again.

I'm on the bench, facing the blank wall, she thought. *The wall is gray concrete. This is the front of the house. The porch, then trees, the yard-turned-prairie, the silo, then the gravel road.*

She breathed.

Right. She put out her right hand, like a mime doing the invisible box routine. *This is my right hand.* She pointed in the air, her eyes still closed. *Water heater, sink, my cup on the sink, the shelf with three boxes, two of dishes, one of old photographs.*

The wall. Grass, caved-in barn, then cornfield. The right hand returned to her lap.

She breathed.

Left. The left hand went out. *This is my left hand.* She pointed with it, in keeping with her ritual. *Small table with the lamp with no light bulb and the tarot cards. Small shelf with two boxes, one of baby toys, one of curtains. The wall with the window.* Her hands came back to her lap.

She breathed.

Behind. The chimney. Her right hand slowly went out and back. *Half wall, toilet, shower. Then wall.* The hand came back. *Grass, tree, then cornfield.*

She breathed.

The other hand went out and back. *Nothing, wall, grass, cornfield.* Her hands came back and met again in her lap.

Colette. Then nothing, nothing, nothing.

She breathed again, deeply, before opening her burning eyes. She looked around. It was all exactly as she had imagined it.

She stood and walked to the window. She reached up. She could just barely touch the glass. She rubbed her fingers across it. It was getting darker, but a little gray-blue light came through. She tried not to think of food. Colette returned to the bench, some kind of old church pew, she guessed, maybe six feet long. She pulled the little table around. The lamp fell off. She left it. She picked up the tarot cards and shuffled them. She held them face down in her left hand and, closing her eyes, drew the one off the top, and held it to her. She kept her eyes closed.

"The fool," she said with certainty to no one.

She drew the card from the bottom, her eyes still closed, and flipped it over on the table.

"Hermit?" she said after a moment.

She looked. It was almost night, but she could see that she

had guessed right for both. The girl smiled, turned, put her feet up onto the seat, and hugged her legs. She rested her chin on her knees and her back against the side of the pew, and she watched the shadows of the world outside darken until they merged with the darkness inside, until it was just Colette and then nothing, nothing, nothing.

Maybe tonight there will be a moon, she thought.

And then she listened for the yelps the coyotes made around dark, for the distant sounds of cars and dogs and birds, but mostly she just heard her own breathing. Just air in and air out. Right now it was louder than anything in the world.

The young man paused, exhausted by the story. The woman sitting next to him stared out, away.

"Well?"

"Well what?" the young man said.

The woman wiped a tear from her cheek, her face darkened, shadowed by a tree.

"The other writing? You said there were two. One in another hand."

"Yes," the young man said, "in heavy, block letters, about the tarot cards."

He recited it...

The man and the woman sat some time in silence.

"What are you thinking?" the man said finally.

"Me? I'm an open book."

The man watched as the woman left the porch without a word and walked into the night. Her steps in the gravel drive frightened two deer grazing nearby. Their necks straightened at once, their ears erect. They bolted in opposite directions.

Father, I have carried these stories, afraid to repeat them, unaware of how they came to me, to my memory. I don't know what's true or real in them. And I don't know which would hurt worse: if these things had happened, or if I had

conjured them up.
Forgive me. Forgive me.

· Chapter 11

Hinckley was no longer a pastor. I don't know if that means he wasn't reverend anymore. I don't know the Protestant thinking on ordination, or even what kind of Protestant his church was. But a preacher never stops preaching. I've learned that much. They may preach a different gospel. But whether it's insurance, financial planning, sales, or Jesus H. Christ, preachers don't quit. Hinckley was no different.

There had been, as there ever is, some kind of scandal. There were allegations that he was taking money allocated for charity. There were rumors that he'd beaten up on his wife, including a medical report listing bruises, scrapes, bite marks, and a couple of broken toes. There were whispers that he'd done weird stuff to young women around town. One story had it that he'd parked himself on a bench in the Payless at the strip mall, watching in those angled mirrors as women squeezed their feet into inferior knock-offs. In another he'd planted himself in a flowerbed, his eyes blinking through a bathroom window, as some lady cut her toenails. Then there was Rita McCarthy's accusation: she'd found his tan leather Bible, his name in gilt lettering on the back, in her underwear drawer, and three pairs of her nylon socks were missing.

None of it stuck. His wife got embarrassed. She didn't press charges. Just divorced him and moved away. The other stories couldn't be proven. And Rita caused a ruckus in the park by the elementary school when she barbequed Hinckley's Bible on her red Weber grill, along with three or four of her bras, in some kind of protest that people just couldn't wrap their heads around. That changed the conversation, for sure. But enough had piled up for Hinckley that his church was done.

I guess, like a lot of preachers, he didn't take to other work, the kind, you know, that required physical labor, and he found other, short-lived ways to augment his inheritance that required not a lot in addition to his charisma, the most recent being The Society.

"As far as I've heard, everyone just calls you Nazis. Is that about the long and short of it?"

His father had left Hinckley some money and a small farmhouse on a few acres half a mile outside of town. I was sitting with him in his study. I peered around at his collection of vintage Nazi and Klan memorabilia. An empty, white hood stared at me from the high, far corner, where it hung from a hook in the ceiling. There were flags, posters, and even what looked like a black-haired Howdy Doody doll with a Hitler Youth boy scout get-up on and a square black felt mustache above its mouth.

"That, Mr. Carver, is a gross mischaracterization of our Society."

He crossed his arms, planting his elbows on the blocky wooden desk, his eyes affecting mock-insult, his lips pursed beneath a wispy mustache.

"Yeah? What kind of society is it again?"

He looked pleased at the question, fished out a business card, and slid it with two fingers across the desk. It read, "society for homeland and independent thinking" on top. Below was his name, followed by the words "founder" and "president." An insignia on the side was made from a cross superimposed on a drawing of a flower, so that, if you looked at it for a minute, the curve of the thin petals behind would, more or less, finish the shape of an oblong swastika from the cross.

"We are a not-for-profit organization for conservative action, social uplift, and sustainable enterprise."

Sounded like he'd been practicing that.

"You want to unpack that for me, Hinckley?"

He fumbled through a few stabs at coherency before eventually landing on the example of his "young men's action group," which he referred to as "the brotherhood," who would be meeting that afternoon. "You should join us," he said.

"Is burning crosses at the Lodge included in your list of conservative actions?"

"While I certainly do not condone that pagan cult, I assure you that we, as an organization, had nothing to do with *that*."

"And what about out on the Troyer farm? The beheaded poultry, the barn gone up in smoke? I suppose your organization had nothing to do with that either?"

"Again, Mr. Carver, as we all know, the Amish, too, are an unpatriotic, abnormal cult, but they are free to practice their primitive beliefs unmolested."

He was smiling.

"Unmolested, huh? I can think of a few ladies in town here who wish you'd practice what you're preaching now."

"I'm sure I don't know what you mean."

He was sneering now.

"And I suppose you know Carter arrested two men, skinhead-types, presumably from your brotherhood, in an all-out brawl with those kids on the square. One of them was the same goose-stepping Lilliputian he had a talk with at the high school. He was distributing your propaganda."

Hinckley's eyes were bulging above his quivering cheeks. Something had got to him.

"Those little monsters got what was coming to them. They know what they did. Arafo is no friend of this community. They aren't kids, Mr. Carver. They're terrorists!"

He spat the last words with righteous relish, beating his fist on the desk with each of the oddly enunciated syllables ("ter-ror-ists"), as if that's just the way you're supposed to say it.

"So are you saying that was a condoned civil action? Or whatever your terminology is."

"Of course not." Deep breath. "No. They interrupted a legal demonstration. We had permits, and they were trying to shut us down and impede our legal rights to free speech. That is all. I don't know what to call it but terrorism" (again with the fist on the desk, though the "ism" seemed to confuse him; he gave it a hard beat followed by a light one and then just put his hands in his lap).

"Your free speech includes the phrase master race, Hinckley?"

"Look, Mr. Carver, we have nothing to hide. Perhaps some of our members get a little carried away from time to time. Zealous, let's say, for the cause. That's all. The Society's goals are positive. We are for something for everyone here. For everyone in our community. We are patriotic. We want what's best for the whole community."

"And I don't suppose your men's group ever meets at the old Hopper house. You know? Where the black girl was found. Dead."

I let that hit.

"There's some symbolism out there I think you'd find familiar, reverend."

I looked around at the swastika-embroidered flags and wall pieces, little Hitler Doody.

"No."

I looked back. He was looking right at me. His eyes wide. He didn't blink.

"And drugs. You all buying? Selling?"

"Of course not, Mr. Carver. Our aim is purity and brotherhood. The body is the temple. One of the brotherhood's main initiatives is public fitness. Exercise."

He split the last word into a three-part staccato ("Ex-er-cise"), and to demonstrate, he pumped his biceps, what there was anyway, three times in rhythm. There was something vaguely nauseating about it.

"Okay, Hinckley. You know I'm not the cops anymore, and I'm just picking at things. For the public good, just like you say. But here's what it looks like to me."

I stood up.

"There's nothing new under the sun. What I mean is this. You're nothing new, you and your band of merry fascists. I think that's what you called it, right? You're running an old agenda that we've all seen before. Your décor is testament to that. The problem, as far as I can see it, is that here, in this town, your side won the battle a long time ago. First through the same kinds of feelings you seem to be whipping up in these boys, but mostly just on the quiet, long-term. Which leaves you with a problem. Your purity and brotherhood bullshit has little new to offer in a place like this. They've already got a version of it that suits them. Isn't that enough hatred and repugnancy for one small town? People here have been white supremacist light for fifty years. And it was full flavor before that. Isn't that enough?"

He sighed, as if I had completely misunderstood his message. I continued.

"It looks to me like you're doubling down on an old set of racial lies. And in the absence of another race to pester, you're lashing out at just about anybody a little different than you are. Anybody, that is, who finds your ideology the least bit repulsive. Anybody who sees you for what you are. Am I close?"

"Mr. Carver! I assure you, you are mistaken" (finally, a three-syllable word he could say normally). "It sounds like you just don't believe in democracy. Shouldn't we let the people decide for themselves what they believe in?"

He seemed pleased, his concern clumped on like clown paint.

"Two more things," I said.

"Of course."

"You mentioned something a minute ago. Sounded to me like Erato, but I don't take you much as one for the Greeks, and you didn't mention feet. Did I mishear you?"

"Criminals," he said. "Arafo." He spelled it. "A-R-A-F-O. Arafo. They are the ones that you should be investigating, Mr. Carver. They're un-American." He paused. "Terrorists!" he spat again.

"What's with the name? What's it mean?"

"I'll let *you* do *your* job, Mr. Carver. As you can see, I need to get back to mine."

He pointed at the window. Trucks were pulling in, loaded with dirt bikes, behind them more motorcycles, a few cars, a caravan of hairless rednecks. I headed to the door.

"Oh, yeah, Hinckley. The other thing."

"Yes?"

"You ever consider using an acronym?"

"Whatever do you mean, Mr. Carver?"

I handed him back his business card, the first letter of each main word of the name underlined, arrows pointing to their combination, written below: "S.H.I.T."

He scowled down at the card for a moment, putting it together. Then just glowered at me.

"Seems more honest. Don't you think?"

Chapter 12

Archie Smith had something going with a Bunsen burner, tongs, and a beaker. He looked over through his goggles when I came through the lab door holding the little vial between my thumb and pointer.

He started towards me, wagging his head, his tangled briar patch-like mane bouncing around.

"No, no, no, no, Hop. Get that stuff out of here. Get that stuff away from me, man."

"You know what it is?"

"God! Yes, I know what it is." He waved his hands around the way a man does when he's pleading for his life. "Just put it away, man. I'm not saying anything 'til you put it away."

"Here." He held out a plastic pill bottle, popped the cap off. "Here. Put it in here. Put it in here."

I did. He put the cap back. He sighed. Histrionics weren't uncharacteristic for Archie.

"How're you doing, Archie?"

He stared.

"Hey Hop. What's up?"

Archie was a chemist or something at the college. We'd met a long time ago through my wife. Well, when she was my wife. Half of doing this kind of work is just the web of people you've got to help you. It isn't like with the cops with all of the rules and departments, the pecking order and politics. A P.I. can work however suits him. In my case, if I land something from a baseless assumption, find enough to make it seem plausible, then it's Carter's job to fill in the holes, test it out, line up the evidence, make it stick. I get paid regardless of the outcome. Archie was the guy I went to for chemical analysis, which comes up more than you'd think. Plus, he knew a lot about drugs.

"So. What is it?"

"It's bad," he said.

"I know that much. I lost a car to that stuff. Had me hugging two Amish men by the time it was done with me, and they were too embarrassed to push me away."

"You took it? That is *not* a good idea, man." He wrung his hands. "Seriously, it's bad. It can do things to you, Hop."

"How'd you spot it?"

"Thousands of those things went missing. This is off the record, right?"

"Yeah, of course."

"I was working this study last year. In Chicago. I didn't know how he got funding with Reagan in the White House. It was supposed to be looking at psychedelics and meditation. Something about researching the effects of psilocybin in a controlled setting. You know, that was what Leary and Alpert and those guys missed when they started out. The setting. And even when researchers began to figure it out, you know? That they needed to control the setting? They missed the *psychological* setting. That was the idea. That with meditation, you could establish a controlled psychological setting, in addition to a clinical, physical setting. But this guy, Benfield, this researcher? He was a nut. He was pals with Nick Sand. You know, the guy with the Brotherhood of Eternal Love. I think Benfield met Leary at some point, but I don't know that for sure. This guy, Sand, he wanted to dose the world. Benfield *loved* that. He was always talking about it. Played around with DMT, ayahuasca, you know? Acid, mushrooms, things I've never heard of. You name it."

"Archie?"

"Sorry, man. This stuff?" He held up the medicine bottle. "This is bad stuff."

"Tell me about it."

"It comes back, you know? Flashbacks. I still get them sometimes. Milder now, but they were *not* good. Zap! And you're back in there. It just don't last as long. There's also a cumulative effect. You know? If you take it a lot. Over time, you know. Works different on groups, too. Like a different drug to each person. Benfield said it was a psychedelic, but not like anything I'd ever had, man. No way."

"So?"

"Yeah, man. Sorry. So, Benfield didn't give 'em the psilocybin, like he was supposed to. Turned out. The whole thing was guerilla research. The whole study! That's the thing. There wasn't even funding. I knew it! Or, I didn't know it. And that was the problem, man. He was testing out this new stuff he'd cooked up. I don't know what the chemical name is. I mean, I can run tests and stuff, but this is the university lab, and there're protocols. I mean, it'd have to be above board, man. You know, Reagan's in the White House. Reagan, man."

"No, it's alright. Just tell me what you know."

"G.M." He said it like it was a code. He looked around. "I don't know if that has some correlation to the chemical composition or what. That's what he called it, though, G.M. Benfield used to say it was God's Mind, and he'd say it laughing, man. Not funny. *Not* funny. By the time it all fell apart, we all called it Grief Machine."

"Psilocybin. That's the mushrooms, right?"

"Yeah. I mean psychedelics are usually good. You know? Like, they put you in touch. In touch, man. There are bad trips and all, and you can't do too much or too often. You know? But they put you *in touch*. Your brain becomes a radio receiver for the pattern of the world. You become the key, you know? You fit into the hole you occupy, and it all makes sense. It's all connected. You're part of the whole. You are the whole. It all makes sense, Hop, man. You see the subfloor of existence. You feel it, too. You work it out. In. Touch. I mean, with ayahuasca, there are some downsides. You know, that stuff can make you purge, but it's okay after a while. Grief Machine. Grief Machine? G.M., man?

Grief Machine is just that, man. You know. *You know.* Catalyst for misery. I almost offed myself, man. And I'm not even that type. You know?"

He laughed for some reason, stopped, got very serious, remembering himself, and then laughed again.

"Why'd you take it?"

"Accident. Vial broke."

"Oh man! That's the other thing! Method don't matter. It *just don't matter.* It's dangerous. It'll get you every which way. Benfield said he'd injected it, just a little, and was spaced for days. Meditating, he said. Said he saw God's mind. You know? But I got a little on my fingers, and was gone for hours. He gave it to the subjects mixed in with water. It's tasteless."

"So, the study. What happened? You said the stuff went missing?"

Archie looked around again. Then tried to calm himself down. He whispered at first.

"He had me and two other dudes, techs, right? You know? We thought it was on the up and up, man. We were his assistants. Ten subjects, Hop, man. Week-long study. Off-site location, which isn't all that uncommon. You know? Dosed five. Other five were controls. They all trained for the meditation practice the first two days. Benfield took care of that. That was his bag, man. Then the five got dosed. None of 'em knew which five, and we didn't either. Double-blind, man. Then they were supposed to continue with the meditation."

"Together. Same room?"

"That's right. I'm getting there, man. Hold on, man. Benfield had this idea. I think he'd taken so much of the stuff that he'd come out the other side somehow. You know, hit some kind of enlightened plateau. The mystery. God's mind. You know? Bliss. You know, man? Like they say if you travel through a black hole, you'd actually see your own back in front of you? Something like *that,* man. Out there. He was out there. *Out!*"

"No, Archie. I have no idea of what you're talking about. But go on."

"Okay, okay." He tapped his forehead with his pointer-finger. "He thought, with the controlled psychological environment, they could get there, too, way out to it. Capital I-T, *it*! But it all blew up. He'd missed something, man. By the third dose. By the third dose, man, it was kaboom."

He mimed an explosion with his hands.

"We'd all figured out which were which. Dose one and two, and a couple of them had to be straightjacketed so they wouldn't dig into their wrists. By the third dose, the five were all huddled together. The three had freed the other two, and they just moved around the room as a group. Like a pack, a herd, you know. They were one animal. One almost got love-smothered by the others, man. They needed to be that close. No separation. You know? One."

"Yeah. I felt that."

"Benfield just never came back. No idea where he went. Then he turned up dead in Wisconsin, man. Weird. Just weird."

"Cambria, Wisconsin?"

"No. Madison. Where's Cambria?"

"I don't know. Somewhere up there."

"Anyway, two of the five had to be committed right away. Mental ward, man. Institutionalized. We sent the other three home, thinking they were cool. You know? That they'd come down. That it was over. I heard all five have killed themselves since. They were so *not* cool. Not at all. The school up there did everything they could to distance themselves from Benfield. I'm not even legally allowed to talk about it at all. I am not talking about it *at all*. That's why I didn't say the name of the place, not even to you, man. They've got long arms. I heard Benfield had ties to military research. FBI? CIA? Deep. Who knows, man. Deep. How deep?"

His eyes bulged at me, like I was the one who knew just how

deep, only we weren't supposed to say it, except maybe just with our eyes.

"And the missing drugs, Archie?"

"Oh yeah! Gone. *Gone!* Thin air, man. Thousands of vials. I don't even know why we had so many. We only needed twenty-five. Maybe a few extras. You know? Just in case."

"This Benfield didn't take them, you think?"

"He took too much, man. That's what I've been telling you."

"But he didn't take the extras? He's not the one who ended up with them?"

"He was gone before anybody else. Poof! Gone."

"Maybe one of the other techs?"

"Maybe. I thought I told you, though. They're both dead, too."

"No. I think you must've gone off on something else."

"Sorry, man. Yeah, Alex was one. Quiet guy. Nice. Died in a car accident. A total shame. He was from Champaign. There was this one time—"

"Archie. The other?"

"Yeah. Isaac something. I think he was from somewhere up by Madison. Bill Matheson. You know him? In biology? He said Isaac disappeared around Christmas. Was it last year? I think it was last year. Fell into a lake or something."

"You got an atlas in here?"

"What?"

"An atlas. Or a map."

"Yeah, man. What's up?"

He got it. I found Wisconsin. Milwaukee, Madison, Osh Kosh, the Dells.

"Cambria."

"You find it, man? Where's it at?"

"Looks like less than an hour from Madison."

"That's where they found Benfield, man!"

"I remember. You tell me anything else about this Isaac

somebody?"

"He was a strange one. He kinda worshiped Benfield. You know? Like a guru? So, he was into Leary and Ram Dass. You know? Alpert. Thought Sand was a genius."

"That's the dose the world guy, right?"

"Yeah, man."

"Was he Nazi-ish? Like a racist? Hitler, Klan, that sort of stuff?"

"That's outta left field, Hop." He laughed. "No, no, no. If anything, the opposite. Like a dreamer. A mystic. I think he *met* Ram Dass. Touched him. He was all about consciousness, man. He didn't see color. Just consciousness."

"So, a nice guy?"

"Too nice. He'd give you the shirt off his back. He'd share anything he was holding. Anything."

"Like a few thousand vials of this stuff?"

I took the pill bottle with the vial in it from his hand and shook it, rattling it in the space between us.

"If he thought it was the key to the door of higher consciousness?"

"Oh no." It hit him. "Yeah, he was *just* that kind of person."

"Dose the world?"

"Dose the world, man. Dose the world."

I made for the door. Archie stopped me as I was leaving.

"Hey, Hop."

"Yeah?"

"This just dawned on me, man. Whoosh. You know? Gordon. Gordon Morris. They were friends. I think they roomed together in grad school or something."

"Dr. Morris? In philosophy?"

"Yeah, man. You know Gordon, right? Him and Isaac? They were pals."

"Huh." I hadn't expected that. "Thanks, Archie."

"Yeah, man. Gordon? Gordon is a *trip*." He laughed.

I could still hear him laughing when I hit the elevator button at the end of the hallway when he yelled out, "nineteen seventy-seven!" Must've been a song or something. The doors closed just as he sang the word "heaven." The elevator dropped down and away.

Chapter 13

On the way back to town, I drove out to the Hinckley S.H.I.T. house again. After all, I had been invited. It'd been a couple of hours since our conversation ended, so I figured the meeting of the minds had to be under way.

There was a banner across the barn that said "Support your brothers in social uplift" with an image of a white figure pulling another white figure out of some kind of pit filled with black, brown, red, and yellow figures. Another proclaimed, "United, we lead to the feature" (I assumed they meant "future"), this one with the swastika-flower-cross insignia in all four corners. A third just screamed, "Brothers!" in jagged red letters between two iron crosses.

There were fifteen or twenty cars parked haphazardly around and motorbikes besides. One big bear of a guy worked the grill. The corners of the white bandanna on his head stood up like terrier ears. His arm hung over a squatty, pig-nosed man with a long, pale goatee. A gang of three oversaw the assorted buns and condiments set out on a card table nearby. Men were milling about, laughing, drinking beer, all in close huddles, really close. Most were inside, on all fours, trying to build something at the far end of the barn, hammers pounding. I walked in. Looked around.

It was a ramp, a big one, against the expanse of the back wall, probably twenty feet wide and as high as the tallest man there. They worked in pairs as little units, pinging nails at the same time, side by side, touching skin, to the point that they were getting in each other's way. Someone handed me a beer. I watched the awkward finale of the project. When it was declared finished, a cheer went up.

It wasn't long before I saw the vials coming out of pockets, one by one, discreetly being poured into beers, others dumped into palms and wiped on necks. Many even massaged the liquid into their brothers' shoulders, napes, and biceps. It was received with groans of pleasure. But they didn't seem zapped into the nether world, as I had been. No one gutted himself or put a knife to his wrist or a bullet in his head (and some were armed). But within a quarter hour they had contracted. As a group, I mean. Their ranks had tightened, so more of them were touching one another, many arms dangling lazily across the shoulders of others. Variously styled rubbings persisted with the comradery. They throbbed to a single rhythm.

Hinckley was nowhere to be found. Some men nodded to me. I smiled back, trying to seem polite without inviting their affection. It was just shy of a normal barbeque. Just a quarter-turn odd. Then came the main event.

Three of the dirt bikes came out and lined up outside on the drive that led into the barn. The huddled Morlocks made a path, and pairs of men mounted the bikes, two with the driver in front, while another man clasped his arms around and pinched hips with his thighs. The third tried an alternate method. The driver, a big, fat man, took up the whole seat, and a long, skinny fella bound himself around in front, like a baby chimp on his momma. They maneuvered the bikes around, engines revving, and aimed them into the barn at the ramp. Thirty or so bald heads pinking in the sun. An army of Curlys, not a Moe or Larry in sight.

I smelled disaster all over this. But I sipped my beer and waited to see what would happen.

The first took off, throwing gravel all over the others, sped into the barn, went up one side of the ramp, and slid down the other sideways, the man in back tumbling behind like a thrown stuffed animal. Both men whimpered like kicked puppies and writhed around in the dust until a huddle of men made its way to them, took them in, and embraced them. And soon the whole lot of them were cooing and purring like kittens.

The second sped in even faster, zipped up the ramp, leapt into the air, skimmed the side of the barn in an arcing half-circle, and landed upright on the far side, descended, and skidded to a stop. The crowd went wild. The men jumped off the bike, joined hands and jumped up and down like little children. Again, the whole herd came together, this time to congratulate the feat with a lot of backslapping and more muscle-rubbing, two men sliding their sweat-slick cheeks and necks against one another's, before they made way for the third team that sat, still conjoined, atop the last motorcycle at the starting place.

The fat man turned the throttle. The engine roared. Or it buzzed anyway. The skinny guy tightened his grip. The clutch popped. And the engine died. The crowd's anticipation relieved itself in a low moan.

The fat guy restarted, and they went through it all again: rev, roar, squeeze, clink, and zoom. They were off, and with surprising speed. They trundled into the barn, wobbled once, and, in a storm-burst of splinters and lumber, the ramp exploded as they crunched *into* the plywood, right through the middle of the ramp, and disappeared, after a close, second crunch through the back of the barn.

It was a nut-house.

Some ran around (I know it's an overused expression, but one, in this case, most fitting) like chickens with their heads cut off. Others held each other and wept. Still others fell and convulsed in the dirt. No one, not one, went to help. If this was the master-race, then we're all in trouble.

I tossed the beer and ran around. Somehow the bike was still zig-zagging, riderless, through the pasture. The fat man was bleeding from his ears and nose and screaming the same sound again and again. The skinny kid wasn't breathing. His face was a mess. Part of his scalp was pealed back, something protruding from one side of his skull, blood pooling around it and running down his bald head.

I looked around. I watched the bike slam into a fence, flip over twice, and hit the ground, with all the angles of a broken umbrella. I looked up at the sun then back down and around at the scattered flock of morons, and started chest compressions. I figured what it would mean for me if I did it, and for some reason an image of the escape route at the bottom of a toilet bowl flashed into my mind when I hovered over the man's face, but I put my mouth on his to blow the air in. I repeated it over and over, until he came back.

He turned over, vomited, and swayed on his hands and knees. Finally, he turned and sat up, his ruined face oozing, and lifted both arms in frenzied gesticulations that I didn't understand. I saw that he'd pissed his pants. He sent up the signal, an animal distress call somewhere between a sheep's at the slaughter and a buck's mounting grunt.

One by one, they took notice, gathered round, and raved in a slippery orgy of hugs, slaps, laughs, rubs, blood, nuzzles, sweat, kisses, and I was right in the middle of it, bracing myself, suffocating, gagging in their young Nazi musk.

In the crush, I saw snapshots of vials breaking, hands glistening, raindrops of the stuff lubricating the tangled mass. My neck burned as hands and more hands patted me, shoving me down. Other hands emptied vials in my mouth, in my eyes. My shoulders ached from the contact, my temples from the noise.

I got an arm free enough to throw a couple of punches, then pushed my way out and disappeared into the adjacent cornfield and ran as far and as fast as I could. I knew what was coming next.

Chapter 14

I'm a boy again. I feel so small on brown summer legs in a toolshed, looking down at the hatchet in my hands. It was a present from my father, whose father gave it to him. A little camping hatchet, a black leather grip. My fingers tighten. It feels good in my hand. I set it carefully on the tool bench and flick on the electric grinding wheel that's bolted to the front, right-hand corner. I'm standing on a stool. Tools are scattered all around. It smells like grease, cedar, gasoline. The florescent tube light chained unevenly above strobes flickers of white light as it warms up. You *can't* remember this. I can't.

I watch the stone wheel spinning, taking on speed. I bring the hatchet head gently to it, just the way someone had shown me. My father? It chews away at the underside of the blade, spraying white, hot sparks in arcs around my hands. They fall like stars, noiselessly joining dust on the ground, one with the earth. I work the blade across. The sulfurous air hits my nostrils. It isn't an easy thing to do well. It takes patience, a light touch. Once the first side is done, the naked metal gleaming like mercury rolling, I turn it over to match the other side to the first. Draw it across the wheel, get a rough razor edge to the blade, before moving it over to the wire-brush wheel on the other side of the axel that spins the grinder.

You know what you're doing. Or I do. I. Me.

This is mostly just for the sake of vanity; someone had told me. The thing is sharp as hell by the time I finish with the first one, but I brush it for polish, to smooth the striations of the grain. And as I flip the switch to shut it off and hold the hatchet up in a striking pose, I catch myself in the old medicine cabinet mirror above the bench. My hand blackened from the work, my eyes gleaming. I feel the muscles tense in those brown arms, the mind working. I watch him wipe the sweat from his tight, dark curls. So much hurt already in those eyes. He looks hungry. I look hungry, angry.

I step off the stool and forward. The mirror takes me to somewhere when I'm grown. Twenty-something? Thirty? I don't know. Before the whole mess, I think. I'm alone. I've still got the hatchet in my right hand, poised to strike, just as before. I'm outside in front of the camper, the old one. You wouldn't remember. I don't remember this. I'm standing there in the gravel, completely spooked by something. Somehow I can feel that I was just a boy an instant ago, that I've come unstuck. I'm here now, confused, terrified. Black hairs standing up on white skin that glows in pale light. That feeling you get, some old, deep, animal adrenaline charge, or like you've been electrocuted at low voltage and it won't turn off? That buzz of brute anxiety?

The ground is yellowed by the lamp near the picnic table, but when it hits the wall of trees and undergrowth there, fifty feet out from where the camper is, everything turns dark. All within the woods is black.

The world contracts around this moment, like it's waiting, and you're waiting. I'm waiting, hatchet raised. It feels like the same one.

I hear something shiver through the leaves in the tree bank. I look up, see a small, white, round moon. Gusts come up and die down again. It hits me that I've been here before. It's Illinois, the little campground I know there. I hear steps in the trees again, in front of me. In my head is a scream.

I silently make my way forward, heel to toe, two steps, glancing back to see the camper door swinging noiselessly. Within is darkness, like an opening to nowhere. *I left the door open*, I think, as I make my way towards the whatever woods, seeing now that pale light is just perceptible on the tops, the little arcs, of the leaves. I can see their veins even. *The trees are alive.* My right hand is cinched around the leather hatchet handle, the head by my ear. It feels good in my hand. I move forward again and wait. I feel sweat rolling into my earlobe.

I hear the leaf-crush again, the sound moving forward, toward me, like in a tunnel. I make the two steps left. I'm on the boundary of where the lawn meets the wild, trying not to breathe too hard. Trying not to breathe. The air shudders out through my nostrils anyway. I can't stop it.

How long has it been? My shoulder is cramping, but I don't move. The low voltage flutter lingers in my chest and on my skin. A new sweat breaks. I wait. The moon seems to have switched sides. I hear the noise again. *Closer.* Then I smell it, the musk of something wild. Electricity all over again. You think, *At least I know it's sharp.* I think that. I squint into the darkness, into the gaps where the leaves aren't. I see nothing. I keep staring, trying to find something to focus on. Like when you're driving in a downpour?

Then I see it shining, a glassine shimmer different from the dull of the leaves. It hits me that it's been there the whole time. An eye. It's staring into me. It's horrible. I'm paralyzed. It moves in closer. *Does it see you?* Then another. Another eye, so close I feel nauseous. The musk fills my head. It's so strong I can taste it in my throat. My arm is still raised. Something warm is running down my arm. We're nearly touching.

The hatchet snaps down hard in front of me and into whatever-it-is. It sticks with a horrible sound. And for seconds, nothing. Then, like it's slow motion, the hatchet handle pulls away. I watch it slide from your hand, wet and warm. My hand. Mine. Movement erupts in the trees, first one way, then another, back again, and away. The world is alive with panic. My arms go out as your legs buckle. My legs.

I run back to the camper, slam the door, and watch through the screen. A shape bolts one way across the open lawn, then another, leaping along the gravel drive, kicking like a bronco. It's a deer. A buck. His legs finally give under him as he falls in the line of sick yellow from the streetlamp by the entrance.

I watch him writhe and kick, making sounds like hysterical laughing. I watch the antlers drop with the head. I can see the hatchet handle, a black checkmark, hanging in the air above. "This is the one," it's saying. An oozing darkness flows and pools beneath the thick slope of his neck. I drop to the floor, choking on his sobs. My sobs. Mine. My hands cover my face. My right arm is covered in blood. I can't get the smell out of my mouth. I just want to wake up. In the mirror above the stove I see a white face smeared and spattered with blood.

When I take my hands away, the tears don't stop, and I'm looking through the Pollock-spatter of dead bugs on a windshield. Concentrating on the gaps. The clock on the stereo says 3:02. People are on the sidewalk. Must be daytime. I'm in a city somewhere. I recognize it, but I can't place where exactly. Books and backpacks. Apartments, restaurants. I knock the rear-view mirror and look at myself. His eyes swollen, red, angry, wet. A few weeks' beard. Hair wild. Cuts clotted with old blood. I drag on the lit cigarette in his hand. My hand. I smell stale beer in what I exhale. There's a notebook in the passenger seat. I flip through but find nothing. The hatchet is in the floorboard, resting on a jagged bed of broken coffee cups, beer bottles. *At least it's sharp.*

I grab the notebook, the hatchet, and a pen from the cup holder. I get out. *Where am I going?* But I don't stop. I'm along for the ride. He crosses the street. I do. I cross the street, and now that I'm on my feet, I can feel the panic again. And pain to go with it. Some kid says, "Hey, man, are you okay?" He looks at me like I just got out of a space ship. "Where am I?" He doesn't reply, just gapes. I shove him down in a flowerbed. A group of women scatters to let me pass.

I look back to the truck. I'm pretty sure it isn't mine. It's dinging. *I left the door open.* I return to heading wherever it is that I'm going, some shitty apartment complex. A motel? In a mirrored window I see my right arm has blood all over it, flecks on my pink T-shirt. I open a gate, pass into a pool area, bump a woman into the water, exit on the other side over a fence. The woman gasps and yelps like a dog.

At a door, sweat rolling into my ears and eyes. *I just want to wake up.* There's a knock. It's me. I'm the one knocking, I guess. I move back. The door parts, just a little, from the casing, and inside is black, an entrance to nowhere. Then four thin fingers wrap around the outside of the door. It opens a little. The hatchet is raised. I hear voices inside. *I just want to wake up.* Everything contracts, but the moment spreads out forever, the horizon on the sea. I just see the fingers on the door. I feel the hatchet in my hand. It's the only thing that feels good. I smell blood. I breathe within myself, in and out. I can't stop it. I hear rhythmic pounding like waves on the rocks at the beach. I feel the electricity again, the hate.

"Yes?" a voice says from the dark.

The hatchet snaps down hard in front of me, and it sticks in the door. Two fingers fall on the threshold and tumble down onto the concrete. I'm not sure which ones. Something within screams. It almost sounds like laughter, like an animal. I hear it bolt away inside, in the dark, bumping into things.

I go on after whoever I'm after, throwing things every which way through the apartment. I find him in the tub in the bathroom. A crop of tiny black hairs on his head. Half-healed wounds all over him, one gauzed over where something is tooching out from his skull where his hair starts. His hand is under the faucet, blood spurting, pooling in the bottom before spiraling with the water and down the dark of the drain. Two guns, pistols, on the countertop.

He's tall. A filthy, skinny guy in a tank-top. Must be in his twenties. Thirty? He looks like a frightened child, his mouth open, gagging on his own screams, animal sounds, eyes almost closed.

Something shatters through a window in another room. Someone. His hollers fading the farther he gets. Another one out the door I came in.

"Oh god! I'm sorry! I'm so sorry! I'm-I'm sorry," he squeals out between gasps.

I hear the noise behind me. More people. They're barking their arrival. *I just want to wake up.*

"Shut up. Turn the water off."

He does.

"Write it."

"What? Write what? I'm sorry?"

"Carver! Let him go!" Behind me at the door.

"Hold on."

I wave them off with my free hand. I glance back. Three of them. Black bandannas over their faces, dressed in black, hoods up. A mini Louisville slugger. An aerosol can, mace I'm guessing.

A gun comes out.

"Write it," I say again, slamming his head into the tiles. "What you have to say to me, write it."

I raise the hatchet again.

The guy seems to be screaming now. No sound comes out.

"Put the axe down, Carver! Do it now!"

"Hold on. And it's a hatchet. They're not the same."

I give him the notebook.

He's whimpering. I throw him the pen. It hits his face and falls into the tub, goes halfway down the drain and sticks out at an angle.

"Come on! Come on! We've gotta get you outa here."

It's a woman's voice now. She's one of the three.

"Hold on, please."

The skinny guy looks at me again, new tears coming in with little sobs. He holds up what's left of his hand. It's spurting in intervals. He's bleeding all over the notebook. It has fallen into the blood-water pool in the tub. A piss smell hovers around him. "I can't!" he sobs. "This is my writing hand, Hop!"

That name in his mouth disgusts me.

Blood pools in the ladle of skin above his clavicle. It's rolling down from the back of his head. More from what's under the gauze.

Then I recognize him. Something in him, in the eyes. I move in close, drop the hatchet, and, crouching over him with my boots on the sides of the tub, take him by the sides of his head and peer into his eyes.

"Think it then," I say, still repulsed by something. "Imagine it."

"I'm so sorry..."

"Shh. Shh. I'm looking for something."

They're tugging at me. I'm holding his head still, my nose against his, my eyes almost pushed into his.

"I'm looking," I whisper.

Then they're on me. One throws me on my face by the toilet. The other sticks his knee in my back and zip-ties my hands. I notice filth caked into the grout, and I fight back the vomit. The hairs planted in the grime come into focus, and it comes anyway. *Like a dog*, I think.

"I just want to wake up," I say to their eyes. That's all I can see. "I just want to wake up."

"I know," comes from the one with the make-up.

"This never happened!" one of the others yells at the moaning bones in the tub. "Got it?"

Some kind of whimpering compliance.

"We need to find Gordon," another says.

They pick me up and march me out. The door is open. Outside is darkness now where daylight was before. Blue flashes, alien lightning, from somewhere far off. It's an entrance to nowhere. It all happens in snapshots. Someone hanging upside-down by a rope from an elm branch. The biggest of the three shoving me through a car door. And everything is black and quiet, and I'm all alone in the nothing, nothing, nothing.

Chapter 15

"Where does the animal stop and the human begin?
Consciousness? Language? Individuality? Where do I end and
you begin? Does the soul, if we have one, connect us? Or does it
separate? Is it a boundary? If this is as far as I go, how can I love?
The early Christians recognized this problem. Jesus couldn't
have been only spirit, only soul, because, while they believed his
love was boundless, his being required humanity. Boundaries.
Do you see? This is what we've been talking about all semester.
So, in one way, at least, philosophy is about thinking about
boundaries. Not defining them necessarily. Not about who is
on each side of them. Philosophy is the thinking. As much as it
can be used to clarify and delineate, its point, its purpose, is to
meditate. To think. Okay? So that is your exam. Think."

Everyone stared at him.

"Now. With your pen. In the little blue booklet, I gave you.
You have one hour."

This was the final exam for the Introduction to Philosophy
class I took with Gordon Morris. He was some years younger than
I was, but I looked up to him somehow. I learned he lived a few
streets over from me, and since that class a couple of years back,
I'd seen him around here and there, and we'd chat. He was easy
to talk to about big ideas. He made it seem exciting somehow.
Like the first time you see a real movie, like a Bergmann film, or
even Kubrick, and you come out of the theater knowing that you
won't see things the same way again. And just like with those
heady films, you didn't have to know anything, going in, to be
changed by the end. Morris didn't litter the air with names and
titles. He talked ideas. Like he said, he wanted to think, and he
wanted us to think. That was the sole course objective on his
syllabus: "I want you to think."

I thought for a minute and started to write what, prior to the class, would have seemed nonsense.

"The moment you begin to write, like I'm writing now, you become split. You sever yourself from yourself. In the present case, myself from myself. You build a consciousness that both is and isn't you, by which you can judge, and by which you can be judged. The written word in this way becomes strange. But it also makes strange, just in the dumb act of being written. And if this is true of writing, it must be true of speaking, maybe even of gestures and expressions. I'm afraid to say it, but the logic of this argument makes me think that it may even be true of thinking. I wonder: is the mind much more than a feedback loop that we can calibrate and direct to zing out like lightning at others? Into the mist at God?"

Dr. Morris had been pacing around. I noticed him standing behind me. I looked up. He finished reading what I'd written so far.

"Good, Mr. Carver," he whispered. "This is interesting, but I think you should keep working."

I nodded, looked around the room at the kids, and they *were* kids (I had twenty years on the oldest of them), and wondered what, if any, difference it would have made in my life if I'd taken this class when I was their age.

A few minutes later, a boy marched up, scowling, handed Morris the blue book, and left, slamming the door behind him. Morris watched the door for a minute, turned his head to one side, fished out his glasses, and opened the booklet. When he walked by, he smiled and put it down open on my desk.

Two sentences: "This is the same bullshit you've been spitting at us all term. I don't see the point of why this class is required."

I was dumbfounded.

He shrugged and picked it up.

"Time's up."

Chapter 16

"Is he gonna be alright?"

It was a voice from the far end of a tunnel. I seemed stuck, awake, but still the math-world was going.

Time passed. There was some chatter, voices around. It hit me that I was lying down. I was on a couch. I could feel the angle of the cushions cradling me. The fuzz of everything in the air, the sounds, I mean, the panic. And then I was awake. The only way I can describe it is like the sound of a gong, but backwards. It started somewhere, but like it had always been going. It grew and grew, louder and louder, until it was everything, and then: whooshp! It all contracted, ceased, in an instant, and my eyes were open.

I grabbed at the first person I saw. I didn't care that he was wearing a mask. He didn't scare me.

I grabbed him, threw myself at him, both arms clasping him tightly. I didn't let go.

I felt his gloved hand on my back.

"It's okay, man. You're alright now."

He let me hang on him for a minute or two. I looked up and saw the girl, her bandanna bunched now between her chin and chest, no longer an outlaw, just a kid. Maybe twenty. She had tears in her eyes, mascara running down her cheeks.

I saw a heap of bloody clothes on the floor. I realized that I was naked.

The man I was holding set me down and covered me back up with a blanket.

"Please!" I said, "Please, don't leave me."

"We know, Mr. Carver. Take it easy, man. We're all close by."

He sat next to where I was lying, so I could feel the pressure of his weight, his warmth, his body against mine. He seemed to intuit the need I felt.

These were the three from my dream. Another came into the room.

"This one I know."

I thought I was thinking it (and in a different word order), but apparently I'd said it, quite loudly.

"Shh. It's okay. You're okay."

The figure got closer. Knelt down in front of me.

"I want you to think. That's the only way out of this. I'll help you, but you have to think."

They all came into view at once. He turned and signaled to someone behind.

The lights went out.

There was a small red blink somewhere in the back of the room. I focused on it when everything began to whirl. I joined myself to it. Until it spoke.

Chapter 17

There were only voices. I'm not even sure which was mine.

"Well, another minute yet. Again and again they manage to cut my rope."

"You're safe now. They dosed you up in a big way. You're not the type."

"I was so well prepared, and there was already a little eternity in my entrails."

"What does that mean?"

"It's from a poem. Rilke."

"Poetry? I thought he was like the rest of them."

"He's not. He's a good man. Thoughtful. Let me talk to him. Let's dig through the poetry, Hopkins, okay? Are you ready to start thinking?"

"Yes."

"Good. Now, listen to me very carefully. I am only a voice. Do you hear that? I am only voice, your interlocutor, a voice in your mind, and all I want is for you to think with me. When I speak, you do not have to believe what I say. You may dismiss me. You may choose to insult me. You may believe that I do not exist, that I am not. All of that is of no consequence. I only want to think with you. Do you hear what I am saying?"

"Yes."

"Then you acknowledge that I am voice, if not a voice of yours, at least a voice that you welcome, a voice to help you think. Is this true?"

"Yes, that's true. Are you the red light?"

"It doesn't matter. Any time you wish to speak, you may do so. I want you to be free to speak with me, to think with me. There is no outside the mind in this room. The room is mind. *This* room is your *mind*. I am voice and you are Hopkins Carver. I am you and you are me. And we will think together. To be free.

Yes?"

"Yes. Okay."

"Where are you from, Hopkins?"

"What do you mean?"

"Where are your memories? Your childhood."

"Illinois. Chicago. I grew up there. Then I lived out in the country later, downstate. Maybe that was after this. Now. I don't remember."

"What is it that you do not remember?"

"I don't remember if this is now or before."

"Do you know where you are now?"

"I'm in the room. The one with the red light, the one I can feel, that's blinking. But the hunter is gone."

"Do you know where the room is?"

"In the institution? Is this from before?"

"Do you know where the institution was?"

"No? Am I still in the institution?"

"I can't say, Hopkins. If you don't know, I don't know. That's how this works."

"I'm not sure where. The past. Somewhere in the past."

"Do you know why you are here?"

"I don't remember. Did I hurt someone? Or just myself?"

"What do you think of your current situation?"

"It's become something of a farce."

"Why do you say that, Hopkins?"

"Because it's... Because it's indeterminate. Because I've lost myself in the patterns, and they make me nauseous, the linkages, the movement, you know?"

"Yes, of course, Hopkins. Do you believe that one can travel through time?"

"Isn't that what life is?"

"I see your point. Has time for you, too, become indeterminate?"

"I don't know. I don't know if it's time. I can't stay in myself.

I'm everywhere."

"Would you say that you experience your life as an unwitting observer: is this, perhaps, what you mean by describing your life as a farce? You can't find yourself in it anymore, in the everywhere?"

"Yeah, I'd say just that. Did I say that?"

"If this farce is truly indeterminate, then you, the primary agent, must carry the whole of it with you, in your very body, every moment. Would you not say that this is the openness of expression without determinants?"

"What do you mean?"

"Well, Hopkins, you are given the opportunity to respond freely to the freedom of this situation, the everywhere, outside of any determinants. You must, quite literally, be yourself, no matter which self you occupy. Do you not receive yourself in each moment because you are unsituated? Because you *are* free. So, if your life has become a farce, has it not also become radically open? Vulnerable, yes, but ultimately free? Flowing like water? Does it not radically unify you each moment in time? With every breath? Even as you feel yourself flowing away? Even as you lose grasp of what you thought was you?"

"I hadn't thought about it that way."

"Why had you not thought of it this way?"

"Because I can't find the past. Mine anyway. Which one is mine?"

"Have you ever been in love?"

"I think so. I loved my parents."

"Did you love them freely?"

"What do you mean?"

"Were you not made to love them?"

"I don't know."

"Did your love depend on theirs?"

"Probably."

"And your father. Was your love for him killed, too, when he was killed? Because he could no longer return it?"

"I hope not. I don't know."

"Have you been in love, Hopkins?"

"How do you mean? I can't remember. Maybe."

"Was it a woman?"

"Yes. Yes, I've found it."

"Can you tell me what it felt like?"

"I don't know. It's all mixed up."

"Mixed up how? In time? In person?"

"Yes, experience, too. Love is heavy."

"It is heavy to bear love, to carry it from one moment to the next?"

"Yes. Sometimes. Sometimes you don't want to carry it."

"But other times it anchors you?"

"Yes. There are times when I want nothing else, and I don't know why, and there are times when the heaviness of it is enough to make me vomit."

"So love is paradox?"

"Yes, from what I can feel, but like I said, it's hard to remember."

"What do you remember? Tell me the story."

"It's dark. Something's collapsed, fallen in. I heard it a moment ago. I sit up in the darkness and listen. I listen but I don't hear. I am hearing nothing. Then something is tapping, quiet as a clock-tick. I throw away the covers and walk silently to the window. No one. But her car is in the driveway. I open the door. Darkness into darkness. No one is there, nothing is there. I walk through it to find the stairs. I descend somehow. I make my way through the house. I'm looking for light. I walk through the house to the back door. I am going on memory, the patterns. A lamp blinks on, but it's cloudy, blinking flutters, tapping like a clock-tick. I move over near the shade. An inverted cone of moths, spiraling, a tornado from the bulb, winging the shade, spreading in wide circles near the ceiling. I cover my mouth. I turn and see three doors, all dark, entrances to nowhere, one leading into the next. I see now that the ceiling has fallen in. There is a mound of wet debris in the floor, a gaping darkness in the ceiling, a giant, blind eye. Something is creeping over my naked feet. I grab the lamp, the spiral of moths trailing along. There are insects everywhere. They crawl up my legs. I feel them in my mouth, in my nose. I throw the lamp at the wall. The front door is open now. I rush out. I'm on a porch, but it's not mine. I sit next to a woman. Her hair covers the side of her face. She drinks from a glass, then laughs. *I know you*, I think. The light from within is blinking. The moths are tapping. I hear the insects chewing through the walls, devouring each other perhaps. The woman laughs again. I touch her shoulder. She's dressed in white. She turns towards me, but her face is obscured, in shadow from a light behind her. 'I know you,' I say. 'I know you, don't I?' She laughs again. I tell her a story. 'I'm an open book,' she says, but her voice is garbled, her face still hidden. 'I love you,' I say, and turn away. I can hear her laughing. I can hear the insects chewing. I can hear the clock-tick of the moths. I open the door, and the insects fall like loose gravel, heavy but small. They are coming through the walls. I shake them off and run into the darkness outside. Two deer, out in the moonlight, walk away from each other and pull the sky apart."

"Good. Very good, Hopkins. Would you say that, in the husks of what love is, that the poles of love or the poles of lovers became a third thing, that they joined, became one thing?"

"I would like to believe that. But it sounds like church talk."

"Why do you hesitate?"

"Because then, wouldn't it be easy? Like a dance. If there are two people, and they join together in a dance, then, until one or both of them quit dancing, there's a dance, a third thing, a one that they've become. If that's love, then why do I still feel it sometimes? Why can I even talk about it, even when no one is dancing, when the third thing is dead? If that's love, then my father's love died with him."

"So perhaps love sits in the space of meditation. Paradox. Love could not be love unless it had already occurred, that is, without its relation to time, to freedom, but simultaneously, that it has been before makes each experience of love, each remembering of love, each feeling of love something new. Do you agree? Is that what you feel?"

"Yes. A visitation from elsewhere. It's grace."

"Do you feel it now, in this moment? Have you opened yourself to the farce of love? Its fluid grace? For your father, your mother, this woman? Love indeterminate?"

"I don't know. I hope."

"Enough for now. Now is time for dreaming. For you to find your way back."

And then the voices were quiet.

Chapter 18

I read somewhere about this mythic scroll. On it is a catalog of everything. That's it. That's the idea. Everything, everywhere, every moment, every second of every tiny happening, of every big one, of every man, woman, child, every creature. I don't know, I guess, any and every thing that could qualify as a noun. It's all chronicled there. Every thought, urge, action, desire, feeling. It can be called up, read, reread, analyzed, poured over, one spliced with another, folded into origami combinations that seem impossible. And the more words that are shared between any two subjects that appear, the more likely is some relation between them.

Think about that. That would explain a lot. Wouldn't it? Why you feel some connection to a place, a shape in the clouds, a house, an image in a deck of cards, a particular dog. To a woman or a man, to a dead writer from another country, to an artist from a thousand years ago, all who, maybe, reached out to an anonymous, indifferent world with their words, their thoughts, their feelings, all who gave themselves in some small, some vulnerable way, to the whole of history, not knowing why, to feel connected, to feel put in touch with something outside of themselves.

That's what I was thinking about when I woke up. That's the only way to make sense of the dream I'd been having. It scanned a million years, a million miles. Offered visitations I couldn't understand, others I could but hadn't faced, all of them running like an old movie, running at random.

This one ended with my father. Not the misery, not the loss, the helplessness, the anger. Just a few simple seconds. I could touch him. I felt his arms around me. The way he rested his big hands on my shoulders when he spoke to me sometimes, and leaned on me, bent over, on my level, you know, when he had something important to tell me. That's all. Just enough to feel, to remember that feeling again. To know that it was there, somewhere way back, somewhere within me, but somewhere just *out there*. To know that it was real. That it is still real.

* * *

Gordon was sitting in a chair reading when I opened my eyes, his glasses tipped down on his nose. The girl at the end of the couch, snuggled against my legs, half sitting, half lying down, was still asleep.

I wiped the tears from my eyes.

"I'm sorry about your daughter, Gordon," I said, still lying there, trying not to rouse the girl.

"Thank you, Hopkins, I appreciate that."

"We're kind of inverted opposites, me and you."

"What do you mean?"

"My father. Your daughter. Like we're stitched to opposite sides of the same spot in the quilt of history."

I didn't know if I was making any sense, or if he knew much about my dad, but he seemed to get it.

"I've thought about something like that myself, Hopkins," he said, putting the book down. "How are you feeling?"

The girl was moving now, waking up. She stretched her arms, the way a child does.

"Better. I'm a little afraid though. What happened?"

"We don't know for sure. You were dosed with Grief Machine. Heavily. And then, we think anyway, over and over. Maybe you found some more somewhere? The stuff is addictive. We can't really say."

"How long?"

"Since what?"

"The barbeque. The one at the shit house."

Gordon shot a confused look to the girl.

"Hinckley's," she said. "We had people there. Observing."

"Three weeks?" Gordon said. "Almost four."

This was not what I was expecting to hear.

"You were with the outlaws in my dream," I said to the girl.

"Not all of that was a dream," she said. "That's why we pulled you out and brought you home."

I looked around. It hit me that I *was* at home. My confusion must have shown.

"It helps with the process to be in familiar surroundings. Comfortable, you understand," Gordon said.

"We call it grounding," the girl said. "What Gordon does. Grounding. He lassos your mind, kind of. Brings you back. He's done it for all of us."

I didn't really get the "us" part.

"The other two with the masks?"

"Yeah," she said, "and like twenty others."

"The Arafo?"

"I guess. We don't throw that around much. The name. But yeah. Just Arafo."

"What's with the name?"

"Anti-racist, anti-fascist organization."

"You're the ones giving Hinckley hell."

She smiled.

"That's exactly what we're doing."

I sat up, rubbed my eyes, tried to clear the fog in my head.

"Who was the other kid? The one I went after? If you're real, then I'm thinking he was too."

They looked at each other. Then, after a beat, the girl answered.

"Kale Rigby. Milky? Milky Rigby."

"What? Couldn't've been."

"We didn't know what to make of you," she went on. "We saw you at their brotherhood party at Hinckley's. You saved him after the thing with the motorcycles. Remember? We would have stopped you if we could have."

I did remember.

"Then, when we were about to raid them, you showed up again. We thought you were gonna kill him. We figured we'd take advantage of the confusion. But then we saw your eyes. Your pupils were like saucers. And then The Society's response. You scared the hell out of them. You know. The enemy of my enemy, and all that? We didn't know you. Not 'til Gordon filled us in."

"Raid them? What for?"

Ever the law man.

She looked at Gordon.

"That's our philosophy," she said. "We only exist because they exist. They rally, we show up. They get rough, we answer it. They raid us, we raid them. When they go away, so will we."

I looked at Gordon. He gave me nothing.

"Marx?" I said, looking from him back to her.

She smiled. Then to Gordon, "He's not like the rest of them." Then back to me, "A little. It's a more Hegelian view. We're on the right side of the spirit of history. Freedom, you understand."

She had his manner down.

"One of yours?" I said to Gordon.

He smiled and raised his eyebrows.

Something else hit me. I wasn't sure if I should ask it, but I did.

"What's the response for your daughter, Gordon?"

He said nothing. The girl answered.

"We've taken care of that, too."

* * *

If I'm honest, I have to say this all scared me to death. You don't see so much from the outside. You never do. If my job has taught me anything, it's that. People, just boring people, go about their lives, just boring lives. That's what you think. That's what you see from the outside. From the surface. That's easy to believe, mostly, because that's what you want to believe. It makes other people less scary. It makes your own indiscretions, your own small crimes, all the more exciting.

I have this theory, just an idea, really. If you investigate anyone, you will find them guilty of something. It's simple. But in its simplicity, it's a genius little nugget, if I do say so myself. And I can do so with humility because it's not even my idea. I kind of stole it from Kafka, from a book called *The Trial*.

This man, Joseph K., is arrested one morning. Before long he finds out that he's presumed guilty, but he never finds out what the charge is. He decides that the only way to respond to an unknown accusation, to the likelihood of being found guilty of anything he *might* have done, is to write an account of his whole life. To draw up a narrative of all of it, down to its tiniest accidents, to sort it out and cover it from every conceivable angle, to see all the possible connections. To, literally, explain himself. It's kind of funny in a pathetic, neurotic sort of way, but he writes about it so seriously, and K. is distressed over it, like the world depends on it. Because it does. The whole book is shot through with anxiety. He's executed at the end. But he only passively resists, with sarcastic jokes. A really weird book.

But here's the thing: he knows he *is* guilty. Guilty of something. He knows it because everyone is guilty of something. It's just a matter of looking through it all and finding it. What am I responsible for? How am I implicated? That's the point. Seek and ye shall find. That's the terror of looking into the dark corners of your own mind, your own life, your heart. That's why it takes courage. Because you *will* find something. There are monsters under your bed, skeletons in your closet. You put them there. They're you.

This is what I'm getting at. I had become a part of something that was out of my control. But, in some way, I knew I was guilty. Complicit. I could feel it, just like Joseph K.

Chapter 19

I wasn't really surprised when Carter showed up and put the cuffs on me. He apologized. It was out of his hands, he said. Milky was pressing charges, though I wasn't sure what else there was in the mist. Carter's always been a stickler for the rules. I made my phone call.

Gordon showed up just as I was being released the next morning. Maybe Burnham had got Milky to drop the charges. I was pretty far down on the agenda of things to worry about. Things had been escalating between ARAFO and The Society, I guess, but I'd been out of my head so long, I'd missed too many moves in the game to know what was going on. I couldn't keep track of what had happened when or what was happening now.

Gordon took me for coffee at Bernice's, after a swing by my place to pick up a few things.

"Liz got the Rigby kid to drop the charges."

"Well, I guess I owe her for that. How'd she do it?"

"She can be persuasive."

"Yeah. I got that," I said. "Listen, I spoke to Archie a while back, before I got waylaid. I don't know that I'm even still on the job, but it's for you. It's your case. So I wanna ask."

"Okay."

"Archie said you knew a fella named Isaac. Archie worked with him and a scientist named Benfield? Some kind of off-the-books experiment on Grief Machine. Kind of connected. Ring any bells?"

"Yes. Isaac Hollowell. I knew him pretty well. He was from here. We were in school together up at Northwestern. Different programs, of course. Roommates. The hungry years, you understand. Kind of lost touch the last few years. Before he passed."

"Look," I started, unsure of how to go on. I tried again, "Look,

Gordon, there's these letters. They're from Father Will. To him, rather. He passed them on to me. I've only got a really loose, not even circumstantial connection, but I think they may be from this Isaac fella."

He was obviously confused, but he sat there and read them through, his face projecting something, but just the edge of it. Microexpressions, they call them. Almost too small to notice. Seemed like he'd gotten used to the mostly stoic Keaton deadpan. The look of a man who'd gotten used to hiding inside.

He finished finally. I'd been through three cups of coffee. My leg was bouncing from the stress or the caffeine. Probably both.

"You think he might've been mixed up in this somehow?" I said when he put the papers down.

He rubbed his jaw for a minute. Looked off, out the window.

"I don't see how it's possible," he said. "He died probably a year before Colette disappeared. I was at his funeral. I spoke to his mom. His sister."

"Up in Wisconsin? Cambria?"

"Yeah. That's right."

"You know he'd lived in that house, or had people working on it anyway? Hopper house? Where they found your girl. The mother bought it for him, I guess."

"No. No, I didn't."

He stared out again. Lost somewhere.

"No return address then?" He said.

"No, but you can do that sort of thing. A lawyer. Somebody like me. People arrange for all sorts of stuff. Lots of them for after they're dead. Old scores. Old loves. Old stories they want to tell. Haunt anonymously. It's not uncommon."

A man on a small tractor, a wagon full of kids behind it, drove across the window. It was a moving Rockwell painting.

"Hopkins. Do you mind if I hold onto these for a couple of days?"

"Not at all."

We sipped coffee in silence for another few minutes.

"You know what gets me?" he said.

"What's that?"

"He's got her down. Colette. That part with her? It's almost like she wrote it. Like she's there."

He watched the muted cars pass by outside the glass.

* * *

The town was hot. People were getting scared now. The Society and ARAFO had got into it. Once at the IGA parking lot. Another time by the high school, where someone got stabbed, another hit with a cinder block. And if ARAFO didn't scare people enough, with the masks, the brutality, the F-you attitude, The Society was just freaking people out. If the community didn't object much to whatever thoughts were left in the shorn heads of the brotherhood, their ideology, that is, they just couldn't make sense of them anymore. The sweaty huddles they crawled around town in. It all seemed like a strange game of Twister gone wrong. They'd gotten too weird. Ruined by whatever the drugs were doing to them. Burnham could see that things were about to blow, that the town couldn't hold much more of whatever this was.

"Hop, are you back? Up to snuff?"

"More or less," I said.

"Can you do me a favor? And it is a favor. Off the books. Under the table. Got it?"

"What's up, Wayne?"

"Phyllis Rigby, Hop. She's gone."

"That don't sound too bad to me."

"No, Hop. Gone as in missing," he said. His eyes were bloodshot. Looked like he'd been up for days. "Look into it?"

"Not sure that's a good idea. My history with that family."

"Yeah, I know, Hop. And like I said, it's off the books. Carter would kill me. He's not too hot on you lately, after that thing with Milky. Thought you went too far."

"Well, I was pretty far," I said.

Chapter 20

I'd been digging around in the Rigby house. Went through her mail, old papers, and whatnot. The place was a mess. Nothing looked sideways though. Nothing but a note. Some kind of shitty poem, taped to a bouquet of dead flowers on a table by the window.

"I feel you in the night light,

Your skin so soft, so white.

Your buoyant hair, it flows.

I love you to your toes."

There was a big smooch of red lipstick at the bottom. Somehow it made me sick to hold. I let it fall to the floor, and the flowers shed their dead petals all over the carpet.

I sat down. Rubbed my eyes. I don't know how long I sat there. I was on a piano bench in an alcove where the telephone stuck out from the wall. I just blanked out there, staring at the phone.

I woke up when it starting ringing. It sent a jolt through me. I watched it ring and ring.

I picked it up, mostly just to shut it up. But I put it to my ear.

"Phyllis? Phyllis?" A voice said.

I said nothing.

"Are you there? Where have you been? I've been looking everywhere."

I said nothing.

"Hello? Are you there?"

There was a long silence. Then, in my best woman's voice, I said I was.

"Don't leave. Please don't leave. I'm on my way."

It was Hinckley. I hung up the phone.

* * *

I wasn't expecting him to show up with a whole horde of morons. Through a gap in the blinds, I saw I don't know how many pull up the long Rigby drive in two packed pick-ups and two more cars besides, one of them Hinckley's Buick. More than a clown car, it looked like something mythic had just broken into the world. A few hecatoncheires out for a drive around the neighborhood.

Hinckley and another one ran up to the door. I locked it.

Hinckley slapped it with his palm, yelling Phyllis! Phyllis!

"Mom!" came next.

It was Milky.

There was a grunting lull in the pleadings for Phyllis for a few seconds.

I checked the window.

Still there. Milky's arms hovered and swayed up around his shoulders as he maneuvered himself in halting, spasmodic gyrations, while Hinckley's hands dug around in the younger man's pants pockets. Milky's hands were both gone, just gone, and reddened bandages gloved whatever was left. The cartoon lump still floated on his head. It looked bigger. He had a fresh one on the other side. There was a wad of bloody gauze pinched into one nostril.

It took me a minute before I settled on an interpretation of what they were doing. Keys. He has keys.

I looked back to the cars. The tangled men hadn't moved. Well, they'd never stopped moving, their shimmering arms slithering in and out, around each other like a box of damp snakes. But no one had even gotten out. Beyond, their shadows crept up. Black figures edged out from behind trees. A van of masks pulled into the neighbors' drive and waited, their heads all turning at once. Two more, a block down, on motorcycles, one black, one white, idled at a stop sign. They looked like cut-outs from reality, negative spaces where people should be.

I skittered around the Rigby living room. Looking for

something. I'd know it when I'd found it. All I could think was that my heart would explode. That I was in the middle of an end that had nothing to do with me. That had everything to do with me. Lungs burning panic. Knives in my temples. Athena would burst out any moment. An owl hooted somewhere.

I settled on the little, black fireplace shovel.

The doorknob jiggled around.

I started swinging when I saw the door moving inward. Hinckley only got out the first syllable of her name before the shovel gonged and crunched his nose. A cloud of soot smoked the air with the noise of the shovel. He dropped like a discarded marionette, a smear of red across his forehead. Milky got a foot in and nubbed me in the shoulder with a squishy, red bandage before falling to the floor, writhing, waving his arms, then trying to hold them to him, then waving them again, all gutturals. I hovered over him for a second or two, the shovel at the ready, as a pool of piss crept out from under him toward the soles of my boots. It seemed, though, that he'd hurt himself enough. He wasn't getting up.

I hit him anyway. His squeal sent up the alarm.

I heard the muffled cluck of car doors and a hundred idiot voices moaning nothing in particular as I ran through the house. I kicked open the back door, a sliver of glass shooting through the boot into the arch of my foot. I spotted the motorcycle at the back of the garage.

It was probably the wet, whistling pulse in my chest, the melting feeling through my arms. The electricity in my head. You know, the panic. But when I tore through the compartment under the seat, looking for the keys, and I spotted two vials of Grief Machine next to my hatchet, I downed them without thinking. I knew it would flick the off switch, even if it turned on something else. I could feel it beginning to take hold as I hit the button for the garage door, footed myself forward on the bike, and saw the herd of men clog a door too small in the front of the house, their hundred arms flailing. I zagged through two blocks of backyards, found a road, and jerked the throttle in the only direction I could.

Chapter 21

The house is alive. The hunter behind it, hanging in the sky. Embers spraying already. My house? Not mine? The door is locked, but it gives in easily. My boots scream and crunch on the floor. Each limp brings another woman's scream. The Empress? The High Priestess? Lady Temperance?

Do you hear it growling, barking? With its teeth in the air? An animal mouth?

There's a river. An acrid river from the gas can. The one I found on the porch, the one gurgling at the end of my arm. Now the screams splash, too.

I can't find my father, my mother. I only find a light switch. It just flicks sound. Nothing changes. The same moonlight. It's low, the moon, the sun. Whatever it is. Amber light plays on the smell from the floor. I try to say something. To the moon? The words go mute in my mouth. There's only the screaming. Please. Please. Let me out.

I hear them coming. Someone from somewhere.

I swing the hatchet in the dark. It grabs hold of something. Tears it apart with noise. The screaming stops for a time. Only whining. Whimpers. How long? When it starts, I swing again. Until I'm worn out with swinging, with the splinters jagging my arm. There's the noise of something dropping behind me, something amplifying the screams. Some mad animal.

Do you know this is your prison?

"I think so," I say to the air.

A smear passes through the window moonlight. They're getting closer.

I climb down a few rungs. Fall the rest of the way. Something glows green and blue. A tiny door to another world. It stings my eyes with the impulse to tear my veins out. To bleed. To die. Escape this.

I feel bony knives already tearing my arm apart, shredding my leg.

The hatchet comes down over and over. An angry wand, magicking corpses out of the dark on the floor.

A flashlight comes on midair in front of me. Where the breathing is. I snatch it away. It's a woman. She's filthy. Older than I was expecting. Chained to a beam, behind a makeshift fence.

"Thank you, Hopkins," she says in a voice I know.

"Where is she?" I say.

No answer.

The woman is already climbing out and away. I hear her red shoes on the ceiling, splashing.

I slip in blood. Mine? The dogs'? Doesn't matter.

I'm freezing. I throw up the hood on my jacket. Vomit into the darkness below.

Hatchet in my hand, its leather slippery with blood. Flashlight wedged in my armpit. I'm back on the ladder. I hear their hooves on the floor already. Cloven, slipping, tapping, splashing.

I stand by the hole, see the room fill with antlers. They're still coming. Getting jammed up in the door.

Fingers tighten, wringing the blood away, the hatchet head against my knee.

"This is my right hand," I say to the air.

I see the antlers swing. The glass eyes on me in the moonlight. I click on the flashlight, and he freezes. Blood, or sweat maybe, tickles through my beard, in my ears.

Everything contracts.

Then they all go mad.

The frozen buck is smashed in the side by another set of antlers. I hear the wet chisel as it stabs between the ribs. Impact rattles in the dark of the corner. Then all around. The herd turns on itself in that room. Violence musking the air with rage, with fear. An animal smell. It hangs in my throat with the tang of gasoline.

I'm on the stairs. Up.

"I'm going up," I say, watching the light's fairy path ahead of me, leading away from the bleats, bellows, and grunts below.

From a window, I watch shadows populate the yard. Bats, guns, rods. I'm trying to get control.

A light appears on the lawn. It's passed from one shadow to another to another. The flames grow, bright moth wings on the tops of candles.

No. Bottles.

One skims through the dark. A flash.

Then the other. A shooting star.

And half of the room I'm in explodes. A wall disappears.

The hunter screams into the room.

I just want to wake up.

To clear my mind, I find the nothing between tree leaves, spaces between the stars, the lunar zero of a moon. Nowhere. Some place to visit. Somewhere safe.

Nothing.

Fire everywhere. Whipping, lapping to its own clock-tick as time moves in spirals.

The hatchet snaps down on a sound from the door. Hunks in behind angry antlers that poke through the doorway. A deer catches fire, charges one of the remaining walls. Disappears through it, the hatchet with him. Leaves a flaming hole.

I climb out on the burning porch roof.

Voices come. Shouts. Something human, maybe, calling from among the smoking husks littering the lawn below. Red lights strobe from somewhere. Roaring black smoke gushes. An upside-down avalanche piles into round, dark mountains in the sky. Something mysterious. Something ancient. Something holy or indifferent?

Red heat vibrates love inside me. All around me. I hear the fat on a body in the room behind crackle with it as it cooks.

My head tongued with fire, arms outstretched, hands reaching, seeking something, finding nothing, I step off the mountain and walk on air.

Roundfire
FICTION

Put simply, we publish great stories. Whether it's literary or popular, a gentle tale or a pulsating thriller, the connecting theme in all Roundfire fiction titles is that once you pick them up you won't want to put them down.
If you have enjoyed this book, why not tell other readers by posting a review on your preferred book site.
Recent bestsellers from Roundfire are:

The Bookseller's Sonnets
Andi Rosenthal
The Bookseller's Sonnets intertwines three love stories with a tale of religious identity and mystery spanning five hundred years and three countries.
Paperback: 978-1-84694-342-3 ebook: 978-184694-626-4

Birds of the Nile
An Egyptian Adventure
N.E. David
Ex-diplomat Michael Blake wanted a quiet birding trip up the Nile – he wasn't expecting a revolution.
Paperback: 978-1-78279-158-4 ebook: 978-1-78279-157-7

Blood Profit$
The Lithium Conspiracy
J. Victor Tomaszek, James N. Patrick, Sr.
The blood of the many for the profits of the few… *Blood Profit$*

will take you into the cigar-smoke-filled room where American policy and laws are really made.
Paperback: 978-1-78279-483-7 ebook: 978-1-78279-277-2

The Burden
A Family Saga
N.E. David
Frank will do anything to keep his mother and father apart. But he's carrying baggage – and it might just weigh him down ...
Paperback: 978-1-78279-936-8 ebook: 978-1-78279-937-5

The Cause
Roderick Vincent
The second American Revolution will be a fire lit from an internal spark.
Paperback: 978-1-78279-763-0 ebook: 978-1-78279-762-3

Don't Drink and Fly
The Story of Bernice O'Hanlon: Part One
Cathie Devitt
Bernice is a witch living in Glasgow. She loses her way in her life and wanders off the beaten track looking for the garden of enlightenment.
Paperback: 978-1-78279-016-7 ebook: 978-1-78279-015-0

Gag
Melissa Unger
One rainy afternoon in a Brooklyn diner, Peter Howland punctures an egg with his fork. Repulsed, Peter pushes the plate away and never eats again.
Paperback: 978-1-78279-564-3 ebook: 978-1-78279-563-6

The Master Yeshua
The Undiscovered Gospel of Joseph
Joyce Luck
Jesus is not who you think he is. The year is 75 CE. Joseph ben
Jude is frail and ailing, but he has a prophecy to fulfil …
Paperback: 978-1-78279-974-0 ebook: 978-1-78279-975-7

Tuareg
Alberto Vazquez-Figueroa
With over 5 million copies sold worldwide, *Tuareg* is a classic
adventure story from best-selling author Alberto Vazquez-
Figueroa, about honour, revenge and a clash of cultures.
Paperback: 978-1-84694-192-4

On the Far Side, There's a Boy
Paula Coston
Martine Haslett, a thirty-something 1980s woman, plays hard
on the fringes of the London drag club scene until one night
which prompts her to sign up to a charity. She writes to a
young Sri Lankan boy, with consequences far and long.
Paperback: 978-1-78279-574-2 ebook: 978-1-78279-573-5

Readers of ebooks can buy or view any of these bestsellers by
clicking on the live link in the title. Most titles are published
in paperback and as an ebook. Paperbacks are available in
traditional bookshops. Both print and ebook formats are
available online.
Find more titles and sign up to our readers' newsletter at
http://www.johnhuntpublishing.com/fiction

Follow us on Facebook at
https://www.facebook.com/JHPfiction
and Twitter at https://twitter.com/JHPFiction